Recent Books by Maureen Child

Silhouette Desire

**Expecting Lonergan's Baby #1719
**Strictly Lonergan's Business #1724
**Satisfying Lonergan's Honor #1730
The Part-Time Wife #1755
Beyond the Boardroom #1765
Thirty Day Affair #1785
†Scorned by the Boss #1816
†Seduced by the Rich Man #1820
†Captured by the Billionaire #1826
††Bargaining for King's Baby #1857
††Marrying for King's Millions #1862
††Falling for King's Fortune #1868
High-Society Secret Pregnancy #1879

Silhouette Nocturne

‡Eternally #4
‡Nevermore #10

**Summer of Secrets
‡The Guardians
†Reasons for Revenge
††Kings of California

MAUREEN CHILD

is a California native who loves to travel. Every chance they get, she and her husband are taking off on another research trip. The author of more than sixty books, Maureen loves a happy ending and still swears that she has the best job in the world. She lives in Southern California with her husband, two children and a golden retriever with delusions of grandeur.

Who's Who at 721 Park Avenue

6A: Marie Endicott—Recently deceased. Was her death really an accident?

9B: Amanda Crawford—The cheerful event planner is everyone's friend.

9B: Julia Prentice—Her unwed pregnancy is about to hit the news!

12A: Vivian Vannick-Smythe—The building's longest-standing resident. She makes it a point to know everyone's business.

12B: Prince Sebastian of Caspia—This royal is rarely in residence so house sitter Carrie Gray handles any issues.

12C: Trent Tanford—The bachelor with the revolving bedroom door.

Penthouse A: Reed and Elizabeth Wellington—This married couple may not be as happy as they try to appear.

Penthouse B: Gage Lattimer—Billionaire. And that's as much as anyone knows....

721 SECRETS

Keeping you up to date on all that goes on at Manhattan's most elite address!

Heiress To Produce An Heir...

It looks as if 721 Park Avenue's society princess, Julia Prentice, is finally taking the wedding plunge. But the real surprise is the groom—Max Rolland! Could the Prentice family actually be allowing their blue-blooded daughter to marry a man who came from nothing? Of course Max has become one of Wall Street's wealthiest whizzes. Sources say that the differences in their upbringings all fell away once the two hit the sheets. Perhaps precaution even went out the window, as rumors are circulating that our socialite is expecting. But didn't we once hear that Max couldn't father a child? Was that a lie, or is the baby-to-be's paternity about to be put to the test? And now with the buzz surrounding former 721 resident Marie Endicott's death, you never really know what's reality…and what's a huge cover-up!

Dear Reader,

Whenever I'm invited to take part in a continuity series for Desire, I'm eager to jump in. This time was no different.

The chance to work with authors such as Laura Wright, Jennifer Lewis, Barbara Dunlop, Emilie Rose and Anna DePaolo was not only exciting, but fun. The e-mails fly fast and furiously between the continuity authors as we work out details for our stories. We talk about everything, from the kind of clothing one character wears to the way another one speaks.

Six women, each of us with different writing styles, working together to build a world we hope will tempt you, the reader, into entering the lives of the people who live at 721 Park Avenue.

In my story, you'll meet Max Rolland, a self-made billionaire who can't seem to get Julia Prentice out of his mind. One night of passion has sent these two on a path neither of them expected—but one that neither will turn away from.

So join us on Park Avenue, in the heart of New York, one of the world's most exciting cities. Surround yourself with the passion and lies and deceptions and finally, surrender to the love.

Happy reading!

Maureen

MAUREEN CHILD

HIGH-SOCIETY SECRET PREGNANCY

Silhouette®

Desire

Published by Silhouette Books

America's Publisher of Contemporary Romance

For Alicia Estrada, as she starts off
on the biggest adventure there is.

You've been a joy all of your life, Alicia, now I wish you
that same joy in the brand-new world you're entering.
Special thanks and acknowledgment to Maureen Child for her
contribution to the PARK AVENUE SCANDALS miniseries.

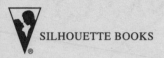

SILHOUETTE BOOKS

ISBN-13: 978-0-373-76879-0
ISBN-10:   0-373-76879-6

HIGH-SOCIETY SECRET PREGNANCY

Copyright © 2008 by Harlequin Books S.A

Visit Silhouette Books at www.eHarlequin.com

Printed in U.S.A.

One

"Damn it, Julia, answer the phone," the deep voice growled into the answering machine, and Julia Prentice winced when the caller hung up a moment later.

She'd been dodging Max Rolland's phone calls for two months now, and he still hadn't given up and gone away. Not that he was stalker material or anything, Julia reassured herself. No, he was just an angry male looking for an explanation of why she'd been refusing his calls since their one amazingly sexy night together.

The reason was simple, of course. She hadn't been able to think of a way to tell him she was pregnant.

"Whoa." Julia's roommate and best friend, Amanda Crawford, event planner extraordinaire, walked out of her bedroom. "He sounds royally pissed off."

"I know." Julia sighed. And she could even admit that Max had a right to be angry. She would have been, too, if she'd been in his shoes.

Amanda crossed to her, gave her a brief hug, then said, "You've got to tell him about the baby."

Sounded good in theory, Julia thought as she dropped into the closest chair. She looked up at her friend and saw the gleam of sympathy in Amanda's gray eyes. "How'm I supposed to do that?"

"Just say the words." Amanda sat down, making their gazes level, which she pretty much had to do all the time. Julia was short, at five feet two inches, and Amanda was eight inches taller. Built like a model, Amanda had short, choppy blond hair, beautiful gray eyes and a loyal heart.

"Easier said than done," Julia said, smoothing one hand over the sharp crease in her pale green linen slacks.

"You can't wait forever, honey," Amanda told her. "Sooner or later, you're going to show."

"Believe me," Julia said, "I know. But that night I spent with him was an aberration. I mean, things got all hot and heavy so quickly I didn't have time to think and then the deed was done and Max was telling me he wasn't interested in anything more than a mutually satisfying sexual relationship."

"Idiot," Amanda offered.

"Thanks for that." Julia smiled. "Anyway it seemed that that was the end of it, you know? Max wanted uncomplicated sex and I wanted more."

"Of course you did."

She dropped her head against the chair back and stared up at the ceiling. "Now everything's different and I don't know what to do."

"Yeah, you do. You just don't want to do it."

"I suppose." Blowing out a breath, Julia said, "He deserves to know about the baby."

"Yep."

"Fine. I'll tell him tomorrow." Decision made, Julia actually felt a little better about things. After all, it wasn't as if she was going to ask Max to be involved in his child's life or even to pay child support. She could afford to raise her baby on her own. So, all she had to do was break the news of impending fatherhood, then let him off the proverbial hook.

"Why have I been obsessing about this?"

"Because you're you," Amanda said, smiling. She gave her friend's knee a pat. "You overthink everything, honey. You always have."

"Well," Julia said wryly, "don't I sound exciting?"

Amanda laughed. "Hey, don't knock it. You overthink and I act on impulse too often. We've all got our crosses to bear."

"True. And it's time to pick up yet another cross." Julia pushed herself out of the chair, then tugged at the hem of her white linen blouse. "I've got to go to that residents' meeting."

"Lucky you."

"I really wish you could come with me," she said.

"Not me, thanks," Amanda countered. "I'm meeting

a friend for dinner, where I will have a lot more fun than you will tonight. Personally, I'm glad to be only a roommate, with no place at those meetings. I'd be bored to tears in ten minutes."

Sighing, Julia said, "Five."

Julia checked the slim, gold watch on her wrist and just barely managed to stifle a sigh. The residents' meeting in Vivian Vannick-Smythe's apartment hadn't even started, and already she was wishing she could leave.

She felt as though her insides were twisted into taut knots that kept getting tighter. Despite that talk with Amanda, the tension gripping Julia felt as tight as ever. She could hardly remember ever feeling calm.

This whole thing with Max had gone on too long. She was just going to have to face him and tell him the truth. Tomorrow, she promised herself, she would call him, arrange to meet and drop the bombshell in his lap. Then, duty done, she could go back to her life secure in the knowledge that a man so dead set on avoiding any kind of emotional attachment wouldn't be bothering her again.

"You look bored," a soft, female voice said from beside her.

Julia smiled in spite of her thoughts and shifted a glance at Carrie Gray. The woman's green eyes were hidden behind a pair of too-practical glasses, and her long, chestnut hair was pulled into a high ponytail at the back of her head. She wore jeans, a T-shirt and sandals that showed off a dark red pedicure. Carrie was officially a house sitter for Prince Sebastian Stone in 12B, but she was also a talented—though currently unemployed—graphic designer and a good friend.

"Not bored," Julia whispered, leaning toward her, "just preoccupied."

Hard to keep your mind on what was happening in the apartment building when it was already focused on something far more profound. Far more personal.

"Anything I can do to help?" Carrie asked.

"No," Julia said, knowing no one but her could handle the situation she found herself in. Still, she added, "Thanks, anyway. I appreciate it. Anything new with you?"

"Just working. Or trying to," Carrie grumbled.

Julia smiled, instantly understanding. "Still getting Trent's drop-bys?"

Carrie rolled her eyes, pushed her glasses up to rest on top of her head and said, "It's a nightmare, Julia. Trent Tanford must spend every spare minute trolling for women, because they're trooping down my hall night and day."

Trent was a notorious playboy. A favorite of the gossip rags, he had a new woman every other day. And those women continually made their way to 721 Park Avenue.

"I swear," Carrie said in a hiss, "these women are all looks, no brains. They keep ringing my doorbell, thinking it's Trent's place. What? They can't tell the difference between 12B and 12C? Tanford doesn't date women who can read?"

Chuckling, Julia just patted her friend's hand and turned back to listen to the rest of the meeting. At least half listen. Hard to concentrate on resident business when her mind was racing in circles.

Julia glanced around 12A, the Vannick-Smythe apartment, and as always, couldn't find an ounce of taste in the place. Everything was cluttered to the point of chaos. It was so gaudy, Julia's eyes hurt just looking around. So expensively tacky, it was impossible to get comfortable there. Which was probably a good thing. Since no one was at ease in the apartment, these terminally boring meetings never seemed to last long.

Just at that moment, Vivian Vannick-Smythe herself, the de facto leader of the residents' group—since no one else wanted the job—clapped her hands to get everyone's attention. In her early sixties, Vivian had been Botoxed within an inch of her life and as a result, her thin face was nearly expressionless. Only her icy blue eyes snapped with emotion. She was very thin, dressed in stylish, classic lines, had short, elegantly cut silver hair and the bearing of a military officer.

Thankfully, tonight Vivian had corralled her two shih tzus, Louis and Neiman, in her bedroom. But even the heavy door separating the twin terrors from the meeting didn't completely muffle their frantic barks and yips.

"I thought," Vivian said once she had everyone's attention, "that before we actually begin the meeting, we should have a moment or two of silence for Marie Endicott. I didn't know her well myself, but she was, however briefly, one of us."

Obediently, the restive room fell silent as each of them supposedly focused on the death only the week before of a young woman who'd lived in the building. Julia and Marie had been no more than nodding acquaintances, but Marie's death in a fall from the roof had made quite an impact on everyone's lives.

Newspaper and television reporters had been staking out the front of the building for days, harassing residents, scrambling for quotes or, better yet, some hint of scandal.

"Do we have any more information on what exactly happened to her?" Tessa Banks, a slender blonde, was the first to speak after the silence.

"Good question." Elizabeth Wellington spoke up next. "I actually heard a few of the reporters saying that the police think Marie might have been *pushed* off the roof."

"That's just speculation," Vivian assured her.

"Did anyone find a suicide note?" Carrie called out.

"Not that I know of," Vivian said, frowning a little. "The police aren't very forthcoming with information, after all. But I'm sure none of us has anything to worry about and soon enough, this tragedy will be supplanted in the news with something else."

True enough, Julia thought as her fellow residents continued to talk and wonder aloud about Marie Endicott. In a few days, the reporters would give up and go away and life would go back to the ordinary.

Well, not for her.

"I have a couple of other announcements," Vivian proclaimed, her voice easily carrying over the rumble of mixed conversations. "I'm sorry to tell you all that Senator and Mrs. Kendrick, long-time residents of 721, have moved. I'm not sure where, but I believe they're somewhere in the city. Their co-op is officially for sale."

More rumbling, more conversations, and Julia slid her glance across the small crowd gathered there. Gage Lattimer sat off by himself, no surprise there. A tall, gorgeous man, he rarely attended these meetings and when he did, as now, he didn't mingle.

Reed Wellington, Elizabeth's husband, sat beside her, but his scowl made it clear he wasn't happy to be there. Elizabeth, too, was holding herself stiffly, her body language declaring she'd rather be anywhere else.

Tessa was tapping the toe of her shoe against the carpet, and even Carrie, beside Julia, was beginning to fidget. Julia, though, had been trained by enough nannies to know how to sit still when you wanted to move. To know how to keep your emotions from showing on your face. To know how to bottle up everything inside, where no one could see.

"Just one more item now, if you'll all give me your attention," Vivian said. "I have an announcement. It's very exciting and I'm sure you'll all be as pleased as I was to hear." She waited until everyone was focused on her before she gave them all a tight smile and said, "I've recently been informed that our home—721 Park Avenue—is up for Historical Landmark status!" She waited for a buzz of excitement that didn't come, then frowning, said, "I think we should have a party to celebrate!"

As Vivian moved around the room, talking to people, trying to spur enthusiasm for her celebration, Julia edged her way to the door. Carrie had already beaten her to a quick exit, but Julia would be right behind her.

"Julia, dear."

Darn it.

Stopping dead, Julia turned, a practiced smile on her face as she greeted Vivian. "Hello, Vivian. The meeting went well."

"Yes, it did, didn't it?" The older woman tried to smile, but her too-tight skin simply wouldn't allow it. "Forgive me if I'm intruding, my dear, but you look troubled. Is everything all right?"

Surprised, since Vivian wasn't exactly known for her interest in anyone besides herself, Julia took a moment or two to answer. "Thanks for asking, Vivian," she said, forcing a smile she didn't feel, "but I'm fine. Just tired, I think. And this sad situation with Marie Endicott has us all feeling the strain."

"Oh, of course." Vivian nodded and her sleek, silver bob hardly moved. "Poor woman. I can't imagine what must have been on her mind to jump from the roof like that."

"So you do think it was a suicide?" Julia asked.

"Surely you do, too." Vivian looked at her for a long moment. "Why, anything else would be too distressing. Imagine. If she were pushed off the roof, one of *us* might have done it."

Julia hadn't really thought of it in those terms, but now that the seed had been planted, she shivered as she sent another glance at the people who lived in her building. Vivian was right. Julia couldn't imagine any of them being a killer. Marie must have jumped. Which was a sad thought. How horrible to feel so alone, so miserable, that your only solution was to end your life.

"Now I've upset you," Vivian said. "Not my intention at all."

She had, but Julia didn't want to talk about this anymore, so she smiled more brightly and said, "Not at all. But I am tired. So if you'll excuse me…"

"Certainly," Vivian said, already looking past Julia to someone else in the room. "You go on home now."

Julia did just that, hurrying her steps down the hall to the elevator. When the doors opened and she stepped inside, she simply stared at the row of floor numbers. She should go home, she knew, but Amanda was out somewhere and Julia didn't really want to sit by herself and listen to silence. So on impulse, she hit the ground-floor button and leaned back against the elevator wall as the doors swished shut and the motor engaged.

Tugging her small designer bag higher on her shoulder, Julia stepped out of the elevator at the lobby and quickly crossed the ivory marble floor. A scattering of Oriental rugs in bright colors softened the cool sterility of the marble and muted the click of her heeled sandals as she walked.

The muted blue walls of the lobby were dotted with expensive artwork and mirrors with elegantly ornate, gold-rimmed frames. The ceiling was high, and a massive crystal chandelier hung in the center of the lobby almost directly over the doorman's wide, mahogany desk. The front doors of 721 were heavy glass framed in gleaming mahogany, allowing passersby a glimpse into the elite, elegant lifestyle of the residents at 721 Park Avenue. Julia had always felt that somehow she and the others who lived there were something like specimens in a zoo. They stayed in their gilded cage while people could stop and stare in at lifestyles so different from their own.

Lots of happy thoughts tonight, she told herself.

"Hello, Henry," Julia said as the doorman stepped out from behind his desk to hustle to the front door. Around five-foot-seven, Henry Brown had shoulders that stooped a little, brown hair, soft brown eyes and an obsequious manner.

"Hello, Ms. Prentice. Nice to see you, as always."

Julia waited as he opened the door for her and held it. It would have been easier to do it herself, of course, but Henry was very territorial about his duties. "Thanks, Henry."

He was still smiling as she stepped out onto the crowded street. Summer nights in New York were hot and sticky, and tonight was no exception. Traffic hummed, car horns blasted and an angry cabbie shouted at the pedestrians ignoring the light and streaming across the street in front of him. A halfhearted wind blew down Park Avenue and carried the scent of hot dogs from the corner street vendor's wagon.

Julia smiled, tucked her bag more tightly beneath her left arm and moved into the steady flow of foot traffic.

After sitting still for so long, it felt good to be outside, part of the rush and bustle of the city. She was alone and yet part of a crowd. And there was a certain kind of comfort in that. Here, she was only another body hurrying along the sidewalk. Here, no one expected anything of her. No one was watching her. No one paid any attention to her at all, as long as she kept moving and didn't slow down the flow.

She didn't have far to go, just a few steps to the Park Café on the corner. Most of the residents of 721 treated the little coffee bar as if it were an extension of the apartment building.

Tonight, though, Julia was hoping she wouldn't run into anyone she knew. She didn't actually feel up to chitchat, but neither did she want to go back to her own apartment and be by herself. She walked into the café and was greeted by the combined scents of cinnamon, chocolate and coffee. The hiss of the espresso machine played counterpoint to the brisk conversations and bursts of laughter.

There were wide, overstuffed chairs, oversize sofas and low-slung tables. Ferns bristled from copper baskets hanging from the ceiling, and soft jazz drifted through the overhead speakers. Julia placed her order, then carried her iced decaf drink and scone with her to a chair in the far corner. Then she curled up in the shadows and tried to be inconspicuous.

Max Rolland's apartment was just down the street from the Park Café and he usually hit the trendy but convenient coffee spot at least once a day. In fact, it was here he'd first met Julia Prentice, the woman currently making him crazy.

He remembered his first sight of her with absolute clarity. She'd looked so cool and elegant, sitting by herself in a corner chair, watching the comings and goings of the other patrons as if she were in a box seat at a Broadway play. Her shoulder-length white-blond hair had been loose in soft waves around her face and her big blue eyes had fixed on him the moment he'd walked in.

He'd felt her gaze right down to his bones, and when he met it for the first time, he'd experienced a blood-burning heat that had forced him to approach her. Ordinarily, he wouldn't have. He wasn't looking for the kind of relationship a woman like her no doubt wanted and needed. But that night, it was as if all bets had been off.

They'd met, talked, touched and ended up in his bed for a night like nothing he'd ever had before. Just the memory of her body moving beneath his, the soft silk of her skin, had him hard and aching again.

Which only fed the anger that continued to churn just beneath the surface of his steely calm. Damn the woman. Why wasn't she answering his phone calls? And why the *hell* was he acting like some moonstruck teenager with his hormones in overdrive?

He picked up his black coffee—no designer crapola for him—and turned to leave. That's when he felt it. The power of her gaze. Just like that first night two months ago.

Max shifted his gaze to the chair in the far corner and there, in the shadows, he found her.

Again.

And this time, he'd be damned if she'd get away so easily.

Two

Max headed across the crowded room, his gaze locked with Julia's. He could feel the tension building in her body even at a distance. Her studied, cool mask of indifference wavered a little as his gaze bored into hers, and he actually enjoyed knowing that he made her nervous.

What man wouldn't?

"Julia," he said, his voice pitched low enough that no one but her would hear him.

"Hello, Max."

One black eyebrow lifted. "Hello? That's it? You've been avoiding me for two months and all you've got to say is hello?"

She broke off a tiny crumb of her scone, lifted it to

her lips and chewed as though it were a chunk of beef jerky. Stalling. He recognized the signs. Well, she could delay their talk as long as she wanted. But now that he had her cornered, so to speak, she wasn't leaving until she explained why the hell she'd been so studiously avoiding him.

He pulled the chair beside hers even closer, then sat down, perching on the edge of the seat. Cradling his coffee between his palms, he stared at her, drinking in the sight of her. So many nights he'd woken up with her image drifting through his brain. He'd told himself he was remembering her wrong. No woman was that beautiful. No woman could be such a stirring mix of both innocence and sensuality. He'd almost believed his own lies.

Until now.

Now that night with her came roaring back, and he saw that not only was she everything his memory had promised, she was more. The scent of her alone— something light and floral—was enough to tempt him. As if he needed tempting.

"I was going to call you tomorrow," she was saying, and Max jerked himself back to the present. With a woman like Julia Prentice, it only made sense to pay attention.

"Were you." It wasn't a question. More of a statement, letting her know that he didn't believe her for a minute.

She got the message, he told himself, since a slight flush colored her cheeks and had her dropping her gaze from his.

"Look, I know you're angry," she said, and a muscle in his jaw twitched.

"I passed angry a few weeks ago."

Lifting her gaze to his again, she shook her head and said, "We had one night together, Max. And when it was over, you made it perfectly clear you were only interested in a sexual relationship."

He laughed shortly and glanced around, reassuring himself that no one was listening in. No one was. Everyone here was huddled with a group of friends or sitting solitarily behind a computer, the glow of the screen reflecting off their faces. He and Julia might as well have been on an island.

"Didn't seem to bother you that night," he pointed out.

"No, it didn't," she admitted, and licked her dry lips. An action that had his body tightening to the point of actual pain. "We both got carried away that night. We did things that—"

"I've been thinking about ever since," he interrupted her neatly, making sure she was filled with the memories that had been haunting him.

He'd never been with a woman so controlled on the outside and so completely uninhibited in bed. She'd gotten to him despite his efforts to maintain a safe emotional distance. And that infuriated him. Max wasn't stupid. He knew her type.

The society woman. Born into a world he'd only entered through years of hard work and persistence. She carried a pedigree and he was a junkyard dog. Their differences were blatant. But in bed, those differences hadn't mattered. In those hours together, they'd each found something in the other that they hadn't anywhere else.

At least, that was what he'd thought.

"Believe me when I say," she told him, "that I've been thinking about that night, too. A lot."

"Then why are you dodging me? We both enjoyed ourselves."

"Oh, yes…"

"So what's keeping us from having another night— and more—just like it?"

Her gaze drilled into his. "I'm pregnant."

If she'd pulled the chair he was sitting on out from under him, Max couldn't have been more stunned. Her simple statement. Her clear, steady gaze. The grim determination of her mouth. All made it clear she was telling the truth. But if she expected him to believe that it was *his* baby, she was in for a big surprise.

He knew something she didn't and because of that one fact, he had no doubt at all that he wasn't the father of her child.

"Congratulations," he said tightly, pausing for a sip of his coffee. The hot, strong liquid burned his tongue and he hissed in a breath, relishing the sting because it gave him something else to concentrate on besides the unspoken plea in her eyes. "Who's the lucky father?"

She drew her head back, widened her eyes and said, "You are, of course."

He laughed. Loud enough that several heads whipped around to see what was so damn funny. Then Max sent a glare around the room and the interested parties found something else to look at. When he turned his gaze back to Julia's, he sneered at her. "Nice try, but I'm not buying it."

"What?" She looked as stunned as he felt. "Why would I lie?"

"An interesting question," Max said, and set his coffee cup down on a nearby table. He silently congratulated himself on the calm he was maintaining. No one would know by looking at him that anger had spiked—along with a sense of disappointment. Taking her drink from her, he set it down, too, then muttered, "Get your purse. We're leaving."

"I don't want to leave."

"And if I was taking a vote, that would matter to me," he said. Then, standing, he simply stared down at her until she grumbled, grabbed her bag and stood up. Taking her elbow in a firm grip, Max steered her out of the coffee shop and onto Park Avenue.

"Where are we going?" Her much shorter legs were scrambling to keep up with his long strides, but Max didn't slow down.

He was a force of nature that somehow managed to part the throngs crowding New York City's sidewalks. People stepped aside, moved out of his way, as he tugged Julia along in his wake. This was not a conversation he was going to hold in public. If she wanted to play out this game, then she'd damn well do it at his place, where he could tell her exactly what he thought of blue-blooded women trying to run scams.

His apartment building was much newer than hers. Less old money, more nouveau riche billionaire. It suited Max down to the ground. The doorman scurried to open the chrome-and-glass door, then stepped back as Max half dragged Julia across the gleaming tile floor to the bank of elevators.

He stabbed one of the buttons and while he waited, he looked down at her. "Not another word until we're alone."

Stiffly, she nodded, wrenched her elbow from his grasp and quietly smoothed her long, blond hair back from her face. He glanced at her reflection in the elevator door, and in spite of everything else he was feeling, desire reached up and grabbed hold of the base of his throat.

The elevator arrived with quiet speed, and once they were inside, Max entered his key card and punched the button for the building's only penthouse. He lived at the top of the world, with a view that told him every time he walked into the room that he'd made it. He was on top. All of his hard work had paid off big-time, and he'd made his dreams come true.

At the penthouse, the elevator opened into his foyer. Six thousand square feet of living space, and Max, but for the housekeeper who came in daily and then left every evening, lived alone now. He'd tried marriage once.

He'd learned his lesson the hard way.

And part of that lesson was the reason he knew Julia was lying to him.

Stepping aside, he waved a hand, inviting Julia inside. She'd been here before, of course, their one and only night together. But damned if he hadn't been seeing the ghost of her every day since.

"You want a drink?" he asked, walking past her and down two short steps into the living room. "Oh, wait. You're pregnant."

She didn't respond to his goading, merely asking, "Do you have any water?"

He ground his teeth together, poured himself a stiff shot of scotch, then retrieved a bottle of water from the wet-bar fridge. Then he walked to where she stood beside a bank of floor-to-ceiling windows that displayed an incredible view of the city and the harbor beyond.

"I'd forgotten what a nice place this is," she said, taking the water and unscrewing the cap.

He liked it. It was decorated in a clearly masculine style, now that Camille was gone. A few rugs dotted the wide-planked oak floor. Oversize sofas and chairs were gathered in conversational knots that were rarely used. A fireplace hugged one wall and on either side were bookcases, stuffed with everything from fiction to the classics.

"It's a lovely view," she said.

"Yeah. You mentioned that the last time you were here." He sipped at his scotch and let the fiery liquid burn away the cold inside.

She glanced up at him. "I don't know why you insisted on coming here, Max. I've already told you what I had to say."

"Uh-huh. You're pregnant with my baby."

"That's right."

"That's a lie."

Her hand tightened on the water bottle. "Why would I lie to you about this?"

"Just what I want to know," he murmured. "The night we were together, you told me you'd just come off a long-term relationship. So what I'm wondering is, why are you trying to palm off his baby as mine?"

Julia took another drink of her water. "Terry and I hadn't been…together like that in months before we broke up. We were friends."

"Too civilized for hot, sweaty sex, was he? No wonder you came to me for a night of good times."

"That's not how it was," Julia argued, wondering how this had gone so wrong. She hadn't expected him to be happy about a surprise pregnancy, but she also hadn't expected him to deny being the father. "When we met, you and I, there was a connection. I felt it. You must have, too. A sort of—"

"Don't make it into something it wasn't, sweetheart," Max said, reaching out to stroke the side of her face with his fingertips. "We were both needy that night and it was the best damn sex I've ever had. But it wasn't more than that. There was no dulcet choir of angels singing. It was what it was."

Julia felt as though he'd slapped her. *This* was

exactly why she was no good at meaningless relationships. She needed to feel a bond with a man before she
climbed into his bed. And that night, as swept away as
she was by Max's pure magnetism, she'd convinced
herself that that bond was there. Could she possibly
have been *that* wrong? Could she have mistaken pure
sexual hunger for something else?

God, she was an idiot.

"So whatever you're up to, it won't work," he said
softly. Leaning to one side, he set his scotch down on
a glass-topped table, then straightened up and moved
in closer. "I don't know what you're after, Julia, but I
know what we both need. What we both want."

"No, you're wrong," she said as he pulled her into
the circle of his arms. He held her tightly to him until
there was no mistaking the hard, rigid length of him
pressed against her. And just like that, her insides turned
to liquid fire.

An ache blossomed between her legs, and the throb-
bing need she remembered from that one night with
him began drumming in her veins.

His hands moved up and down her spine, sending
tingling shards of awareness through her body, and
suddenly, Julia couldn't breathe. Couldn't concentrate.
Couldn't quite remember that she'd planned to say no
to him. To tell him that sex without commitment wasn't
what she was looking for.

He leaned down, brushed his mouth over hers and
then pulled back, his gaze meeting hers, his eyes
shining with a raw hunger that shook her to her core.

"Tell me now," he whispered. "If you mean no, say it now and I'll stop."

Say it! her brain ordered.

But just as quickly, her body took over. There was no future with Max. He didn't believe her about their baby. And to prove it to him with a paternity test, she'd have to wait until the child was born. So there was no convincing him. If she had half a brain, she'd walk out of this gloriously appointed apartment, away from this man with his near magical touch and console herself with the fact that she'd done the right thing. She'd told him about the baby. It was his choice to not believe her.

But she didn't want to go.

She wanted another night.

Every square inch of her body was clamoring for it. Every beat of her heart made the need for him more desperate. So she made another decision that would no doubt come back to haunt her.

"I'm not saying no," she said, and lifted her hands to his chest. She ran her palms across his open-collared dress shirt and felt the hard muscles beneath.

He drew in a long, deep breath, then let her go just enough to slide his hands to her breasts. Through the fine linen, he cupped her and ran his thumbs across her hardened nipples. The lacy bra she wore was not enough to keep the heat of his touch from seeping into her skin.

"Then say yes," he demanded, squeezing her breasts a little harder, just enough to make her need him even more.

"Yes, Max. Damn you, *yes*."

Triumph shone in his eyes briefly, before he took her mouth with his again. The moment his lips touched hers, Julia closed her eyes on a sigh of surrender. Heat spiraled through her, burning through her veins, electrifying every cell. His tongue parted her lips and she took him inside, tangling her tongue with his in an erotic dance of expectation.

While he kissed her, his hands moved quickly, surely, to the buttons of her blouse. In seconds, they were open and her shirt was dropping off her arms to lie on the floor. Her bra came next and then his hands were on her breasts, stroking, rubbing, squeezing. His fingers tugged at her nipples all the while his mouth drove her insane with a need that nearly swamped her.

He broke the kiss abruptly and bent to take first one nipple, then the other into his mouth. His tongue and lips and teeth worked her flesh, playing her body as if she were a finely tuned instrument. Higher and higher she flew, and as she cupped the back of his head, holding his mouth to her, her eyes opened to slits. She stared out at the breadth of Manhattan, sprawled out below them, and the lights of the city blurred into a kaleidoscope of color.

"More," he whispered against her skin.

"Yes, Max, more. Please, more." She'd never felt as she did when she was with him. This one man was to her body what a lit match was to a stick of dynamite. Why was he the only one who could create such incredible sensations?

His fingers deftly undid the button and zipper of her slacks and he slid them down the length of her legs, tugging her lacy thong down at the same time. The cool air of the room kissed her skin and she shivered. She wasn't cold, though. How could she ever be cold while Max's hands were on her flesh?

"Hold on to me." He knelt in front of her and waited until her hands fell to his broad, muscular shoulders. Then he lifted her right leg, laid it across his back and looked up at her.

Desire, passion and more glittered in his eyes and Julia felt caught in that steady, studying gaze of his. She trembled as, keeping his gaze locked with hers, he moved closer and inched his mouth toward the aching center of her. With his fingers, he parted the pale blond curls at the tops of her thighs, and Julia sucked in a gulp of air, capturing it in her lungs as if afraid she might never draw another.

But that stolen breath flew out of her in a rush the moment his tongue touched her most intimate flesh. He closed his eyes, leaned into her and began to gently torture her with clever strokes and long, damp caresses. Julia curled her fingers into his shirt and hung on for all she was worth. Her balance was precarious, but she wouldn't have moved for all the money in the world.

She wanted to be just like this forever. To have the feel of his mouth on her, the warmth of his tongue, the brush of his breath, the slide of his fingers as he pushed first one, then two up and inside her.

"Max!" She swayed and he used his free arm to

steady her. To hold her tightly in position so that he could continue his gentle invasion.

As his fingers moved in and out of her body, his mouth continued its delicious torture. He tasted and teased, built her internal fire into a conflagration, then eased back before she could burst into flame. He kept her on the edge of release, teetering dangerously close, but always just a breath away.

Julia's body was a quivering mass of need and raw passion. She held on to him and rocked her hips against him as best she could. Her eyes opened again and she looked down at him as he took her, drove her, faster and faster until breathing was a memory and the only thing that mattered was the shattering climax that remained just out of reach.

"Max, please," she whispered, her words broken. "Please, now. Now."

His mouth pushed her onward, his fingers dancing in and out of her body, keeping time with the stroke of his tongue. And when she knew she couldn't take another moment, Max gave her that one last stroke that sent her tumbling into oblivion, the only steady point in the universe being his shoulders beneath her hands.

Before the last tremor had coursed through her system, Julia was swung up into his arms. He looked down at her and she saw on his features the rigid control he was maintaining. She lifted one hand, cupped his cheek and said, "More, Max. I want you inside me."

"You'll have me," he promised, already striding across the wide room toward a hall. Down that hall, his footsteps sounded out like a frantic heartbeat against the shining wood floor.

Julia couldn't tear her gaze from him, drinking in the strong line of his jaw. The way his dark hair fell across his forehead. The shine in his grass-green eyes. Her body quickened, already needing him again.

His bedroom was a massive space, lit only by the moon and the city lights below. A bed big enough to comfortably sleep six sat positioned opposite the wall of windows. A red silk duvet was already pulled down and when Max dropped her onto the mattress, she felt as if she was surrounded by softness.

She watched, speechless, as he quickly tore off his clothes. Her gaze dropped to the hard, thick length of him, and everything in her tingled. Lifting her arms to him, she welcomed him to her and when he covered her body with his, Julia luxuriated in the feel of his flesh aligned with hers. Rough to smooth, their bodies moved against each other as if made for this and nothing more.

His touch sent her spinning again, whirling with emotions, sensations too many to identify. She didn't try. Instead, she concentrated solely on being with him, and when he rolled onto his back and drew her atop him, Julia went willingly, eagerly.

How had they come to this? she wondered. That one magical night with him had created life. Life he didn't believe in or care about. Life that she looked forward to nurturing.

Two strangers they'd been and really still were. And yet, here in this room, on this bed, she felt as if she'd known him forever. As if a part of her had always been waiting for him to walk into her life. As if her body recognized his.

His hands clamped her upper thighs as she rose above him. His mouth curved into a lazy smile and Julia couldn't quite resist bending over him to kiss that mouth. Her hair fell on either side of them, a soft, blond curtain, shutting out everything but the two of them.

Mouths met, tongues twisted together and breath mingled, as if they were one. As if this was somehow meant to be. But before she could give that thought any more consideration, he lifted her hips and slowly, expertly, guided her down atop him.

Julia straightened, arched her back and hissed in a breath as he slowly, inexorably filled her. His hard length pushed into her heat and she took him deeply within. She was impaled on him and felt his body claim hers completely.

Staring down into his eyes, Julia sighed and wiggled her hips, grinding her body to his, and her reward was watching his eyes wheel.

"My turn," she whispered, her voice a mere hush as her body began to move on his. She rocked her hips, she twisted and arched her back. She ran her hands up and down his chest, scraping her short, even nails along his skin, across his flat nipples.

He groaned and fixed his gaze on her as if he didn't dare look away. As if nothing in the world was more important to him in that moment than she was. And it was a heady feeling. Julia kept her gaze locked with his as she lifted her hands, sliding them up her own body to cup her breasts.

As he watched, she tweaked her own nipples, and in the flare of excitement in his eyes, she felt her own eagerness build. She'd caught him, trapped him in her web now, and it was he who had to do nothing but to accept. To feel. To take that slippery climb to completion.

Pure, feminine power roared through her as Julia watched Max's fixed gaze. She read his hunger, saw his need, felt his passion. Smiling, she lifted both arms high over her head, arched her back again and rode him harder, faster. Her hips bucked and her soft moans murmured into the darkness. His hands at her hips tightened until she felt the sting of each fingertip burning into her skin.

Then he slid one hand down to the point where their bodies were joined. He touched her. That one incredibly sensitive piece of flesh. He found that one spot and stroked it as she rocked on him, and in seconds, he'd turned the tables. Now it was Julia again, clamoring, breathlessly racing toward the peak awaiting them.

When she screamed his name and shattered in his grasp, she heard his own hoarse cry echo hers an instant later. Then his arms came around her, and holding her tightly, Max cushioned their fall back to earth.

Three

With Julia curled up beside him, Max drew his first easy breath in two months. He finally had her back where he wanted her. He wasn't sure what she was trying to pull with this baby ruse, but whatever it was, he'd find out. Now that she was back in his bed where she belonged.

He wasn't an idiot. He knew damn well she'd enjoyed herself every bit as much as he had. So what was the point of the lies? he wondered. What could she possibly be after?

Going up on one elbow, he looked down into her eyes, gave her a half smile and said smugly, "Now do you want to try to tell me you're not interested in a sexual relationship?"

Her wide blue eyes narrowed perceptibly as she met his gaze. "What I said was, I'm not interested in a *solely* sexual relationship."

"I think you just proved that wrong. In a spectacular way, from my perspective."

Muttering something he didn't quite catch, she shoved herself away from him and scooted off the edge of the bed. Naked, she was enough to make his mouth water. Her build was small, almost fragile, but toned. She had strength in her slightly too-thin frame, and as she stalked around the edge of the bed headed for the living room, Max could freely admit that he wanted her. Again.

Quietly, he slipped out of bed and followed her, his bare feet making no sound on the floor. He watched as she bent down to scoop up her clothing, then he leaned one shoulder against the doorjamb and watched as she quickly got dressed.

"What's your hurry?"

She flashed him a look, sucked in a gulp of air and said, "I didn't come here for *this*."

"Maybe not, but we're damn good at it. Why not do it again?"

"Because," she said, tugging her panties and then her slacks up and over her legs, "there's no point."

"You screamed," he said with a satisfied grin. "I think that's the point."

Scowling at him, she tossed her blond hair behind one shoulder, slipped her bra on and clumsily hooked it into place. "There's no talking to you, is there?"

"If you want to talk, we'll talk." He walked toward her, comfortable with his own nudity. She, however, looked a little nervous at the fact that he was still naked. Good. He was a man who liked knowing he had the advantage of his opponent. And no matter how else he could describe their "relationship," *opponent* was definitely part of the mix.

"You could start with why you're trying to convince me you're pregnant."

She kept her gaze determinedly fixed on his. "I *am* pregnant," she said. "I only told you because it was the right thing to do."

"Oh, concerned about doing the right thing, are you?"

"Honestly?" she countered. "It's becoming less and less important to me with every word you say."

She slipped her white blouse on and before she could button it, Max was there, hands at her shoulders. He pulled her in tightly to him, looked down into her eyes and asked quietly, "What is this really about?"

For one moment, he thought he read disappointment in her eyes, but then that moment passed and her eyes were once again a cool, dispassionate blue. "You don't believe me, so why should I bother trying to convince you?"

A niggling doubt began to chew at the back of his mind, but he set it aside quickly. It didn't matter what she said. He already knew the truth. "I want to know who told you to try this," he said.

"What?"

"Word get out that I wanted an heir, is that it?" His fingers tightened on her shoulders briefly.

"I don't know what you're talking about."

"Please. We both know that salacious gossip is your society's life blood. The rich and spoiled's rumor mills put even Hollywood to shame."

She stepped back out of his grasp and Max let her go. Tidily, she did up the buttons on her shirt, scooped her hair back from her face and finger-combed it until it looked less like she'd just rolled out of bed with her lover. Then she turned away, picked up her bag from where she'd dropped it earlier and stepped into her sandals.

Only when she was ready to leave did she turn back to him again. "Believe what you will, Max. But I told you the truth."

"As you see it, of course."

"Isn't that the only way any of us see it?"

He frowned after her, but he let her go and didn't try to stop her when she stepped into the elevator and left.

"I'm an idiot," Julia groaned to Amanda an hour later as she dropped her head onto the back of the couch. Her body was still humming from Max's touch, and her temper was still simmering with the sting of his distrust. Why would he simply assume she was lying? For heaven's sake, he didn't even ask for a paternity test!

She closed her eyes, opened them again and looked around her apartment. She'd built a little nest here, a

place where she felt comfortable. Happy. The walls
were a soft mauve, the window treatments sheer white
and the overstuffed couch and love seat were covered
in ivory spattered with cabbage roses. In this apartment, Julia had finally made a home for herself.

Unlike the places she'd grown up, there was nothing
cold or formal or rigid here. She always felt at ease
here—until tonight. And that was her fault as much as
it was Max's.

Staring up at the ceiling, she said, disbelief coloring
her tone, "I went right back to bed with him. It's like
he can hypnotize me or something."

"Lucky you," Amanda said.

"Lucky?" Julia shook her head. "It's like an out-of-
body experience or something, except I'm right there
in my body. I just don't have control over it anymore."
She slapped one hand over her eyes. "For pity's sake,
we didn't even use a condom. *Again*."

"A little late to be worrying about protection, don't
you think?"

"I'm *not* thinking. That's the solid truth. It's like my
brain shuts down when he touches me. I don't understand this at all."

"Why try to understand it?" Amanda said on an
envious sigh. "Just enjoy it."

"You're not helping." Julia turned her head to glare
at her best friend, seated cross-legged on the love seat
opposite her.

"What do you want me to say?" Amanda laughed
and dipped her spoon into the pint of chocolate-chip ice

cream. "Oooh. Bad Julia. Having sex. Shame." She took a bite, smiled and shook her head. "Not gonna happen."

"But he didn't believe me about the baby."

Amanda frowned, leaned forward and picked up the other carton of ice cream, already open, a spoon jutting up from its frozen heart. Handing it to Julia, she said, "Okay, that's terrible. He should have believed you. I've never met anybody as scrupulously honest as you."

Julia took a bite of her strawberry ice cream, let the frozen sugar dissolve on her tongue and then said, "You should tell him that. He didn't even consider what I was saying. Just flat out called me a liar."

"And then to get back at him for that insult, you had sex with him." Amanda laughed. "That'll teach him."

Julia grimaced, picked up a pink, ruffled throw pillow and tossed it at her friend. "I already said I'm an idiot."

Still chuckling, Amanda asked, "The question is, was it worth it?"

"Oh, God," Julia said on a sigh. "The man has magic fingers. And a magic mouth and a magic—"

"I get the picture. And color me jealous." Amanda stabbed at her ice cream, scooped up a huge bite and ate it.

Julia winced. She shouldn't be going on and on about Max and the incredible sex. Wasn't Amanda here, living with her, because her own romance had ended badly? "I'm sorry, sweetie," she said guiltily.

"Oh, don't be," Amanda said, lifting her chin. "Not

on my account, anyway. Yes, I loved a loser, but that's over now. I'm good. Perfectly content with my choco-late-chip ice cream and vicarious thrills through you."

"Humph. Those thrills have come to an end," Julia said, hoping that her firm tone would even convince herself. "I can't do this with Max again, Amanda. Sex isn't enough."

"Hmm. Won't convince me of that at the moment."

"Don't I have enough problems?" Julia countered. "What am I supposed to do?"

Setting her ice cream down on the table in front of her, Amanda looked at her friend and said, "You're the only one who can decide that, Jules. It's your baby. Your life. What do you want to do?"

The answer to that question was easy and compli-cated in turns. She wanted her baby. But she was terri-fied of what would happen in the coming months.

Sighing, she said, "You know I always wanted kids."

"True."

"But I'd expected to be married first."

"Naturally, but things don't always go in order, either."

"I want the baby," Julia said. "But what happens when people find out about it?"

"Honey, this isn't the fifties. Times have changed."

"Times maybe," Julia acknowledged. "But my family hasn't. You know my parents."

Amanda shuddered. "Good point. They wouldn't exactly throw a party, would they."

"To say the least." She stopped for a moment and

imagined having this little chat with her parents. She could almost *feel* their disapproval. Their shame. Their complete distaste for what she'd done and who she was.

The elder Prentices' only concern was how things looked. If they found out their only child was pregnant and unmarried, they'd do everything they could to make her life a living hell. True, they couldn't force her to get an abortion, but they'd surgically slice her out of their lives—and as bad as they were, they were her only family. Could she really stand being tossed aside?

Julia shivered and pushed those thoughts aside. "It's not just my parents to consider, either. What about all the old-line charities I raise funds for? You think they're going to appreciate the 'unwed mother' thing?"

"Your family will get over it," Amanda said with more certainty than Julia felt. "As for the rest, you'll deal with it as it comes."

"Easier said than done."

"If you want this baby," Amanda said reasonably, "what choice do you have?"

By morning, Julia was still thinking about her friend's question. All night long, she'd been plagued by nightmares. She could still feel the panic she'd experienced in her sleep as she'd run down long, dark streets, empty of people, but filled with shadows. She'd held her baby in her arms, and the infant's wails had echoed off the buildings on either side of her. Rain stained the streets, and her frantic gaze couldn't find a single person to help her.

To befriend her.

She shivered a little, shoved aside the remnants of the dream and cupped both hands around her mug of hot tea, hoping the heat would seep into her bones. She squinted into the bright spear of sunlight slanting in through the windows and told herself that dreams were not reality.

Besides, this was ridiculous, and she knew it. Here she was, twenty-eight years old, a college graduate, with a steady income, her own home and a select group of good friends. So she was pregnant and not married? What was the big deal? Other women faced this problem all the time. Why was she making such a mountain out of her own personal molehill?

"Are you that big a coward?" she asked herself and was half-afraid of the answer.

"Mail's here." Amanda strode into the breakfast room, dropped a stack of envelopes onto the table and headed for her bedroom "I've got an appointment with a nervous bride in about an hour. Her prospective mother-in-law is trying to arrange the wedding *her* way. Hello, red flag, blushing bride! Run for the hills!" She shrugged, grinned and said, "Should be interesting."

As an event planner, Amanda was always rushing to and from meetings with clients, suppliers and site committees. She was wearing a dark red business suit that looked amazing on her. As she walked away, she smiled over her shoulder and said, "Let me know if there's anything in that stack for me."

Julia dutifully flipped through the envelopes. Bills,

circulars, party invitations… She stopped when she came to one without a stamp or postmark. It was addressed to Julia Prentice, but there was no street address on the envelope, only her name. Frowning, she broke the seal, took out the single sheet of paper and read the all-too-brief message.

Ms. Prentice—I know about your baby. If you don't want the world to know, wire one million dollars to this Grand Cayman account. You have one week to comply.

There was an account number listed below the message, but obviously, no signature. A blackmail letter? Julia's hands shook, then fisted on the single page of paper. Who was behind this? Someone in the building? Someone she thought of as a friend? Apart from herself, no one but Amanda and Max knew about the baby. Max didn't believe her about it, and Amanda would never betray her.

So how had this…person found out? Had someone been listening at the Park Café? Had she been overheard despite her attempts to keep her conversation quiet? Concentrating, despite the rush of adrenaline inside her, she racked her brain, trying to remember the faces of the other patrons at the café the night before. But she couldn't. She'd been too engrossed in her own thoughts. Too wrapped up in her own world and situation to take note of anyone else around her. And truth to tell, once Max had shown up, the building could have been on fire and she'd only have seen Max's eyes.

"Oh, God."

She dropped the letter to the table, slapped one hand to her mouth and fought for air as she suddenly found it hard to breathe. What was she going to do? She didn't have the kind of disposable income that would allow her to pay out a million dollars in cash. And she couldn't stand the thought of her private business being the subject of titillating gossip or speculation.

"Sweetie?" Amanda's voice cut through the clamoring noise in her mind and Julia looked up through tear-glazed eyes at her friend. "What is it, Jules? What happened?"

Julia glanced at the letter and Amanda snatched it up and read it.

"Damn! Who would do something like—" She broke off and said, "Never mind. What are you going to do about this?"

"I don't know."

"You should go to the police, Jules."

"What good would that do?" She shook her head and fought to think clearly, to fight down the panic already clawing through her. Her stomach was churning, her heart was pounding and her mouth was dry.

"Blackmail's a crime."

"I know that," Julia said softly. "But what can the police do about it? Find the blackmailer? Would that stop whoever it is? They'd still leak my secret."

"It won't be a secret forever, sweetie," Amanda

reminded her gently. "People are going to find out you're pregnant. It's not really something you can hide."

"Yes, but they'll find out when *I'm* ready. Not when some malicious bastard decides to throw me to the gossip wolves. I can't let my parents find out about this from reading it in the papers. And I can't tell them myself yet, either."

"So what *are* you going to do?"

Julia pushed up out of her chair, walked a few steps, then turned around to look at the other woman. "I can't go to my parents with this. And I can't pay the blackmail myself. There's really only one thing I *can* do," she said. "I have to go to Max."

Max sat at his desk, trying to focus on the day's activities. Keeping his finger on Wall Street's pulse was the secret of his success. He had an innate ability to see which way the market would roll. To make his move before others had even considered the situation in front of them.

His reputation was such that his advice was taken as golden, and his rivals kept a close watch on him in hopes of getting the jump on him. Which hadn't happened. Max enjoyed his work. Enjoyed being the best. He relished the swings, the ups and downs, of the market and delighted at defeating it, bending it to his own whims.

But today, he couldn't focus. Couldn't make himself care about oil prices or hog futures or any other damn thing on the screens. Today, all he could think of was Julia.

He hadn't slept because his bed smelled of her. He closed his eyes and he could feel her body on his. His mind continued to dredge up image after image of her. Her blond hair mussed, tangled, her eyes soft and wide, or glittering with passion. Her mouth, full and delectable as she rose over him, took him inside.

The damn woman was haunting him.

He sat back in his office chair, swiveled it around to turn his back on the view of Manhattan and, instead, swept his gaze around his office. The room was big, the furniture was black, chrome and glass, and the atmosphere quietly successful. When he held meetings in here, this room was enough to put his adversaries on the defensive. This room said plainly that Max Rolland was a man to be taken seriously. With a lot of caution.

His world was exactly the way he'd always dreamed it would be. He had money. He had prestige. He had the whole city by the damn tail. What he didn't have was a family. A son. An heir.

Jumping out of the black leather chair, he stalked across the room, poured himself a cup of coffee from the silver urn atop the wet bar and took a long sip while his thoughts raced. He'd married Camille, fully expecting to build the family dynasty he'd always planned on.

She'd had good bloodlines. She would have given his children the pedigree they deserved and he would have given them what they needed to excel in the world he'd wanted to hand down to them.

"Best-laid plans," he muttered darkly, letting himself remember, however briefly, the look on Camille's face the last time he'd seen her.

She'd looked at him with pity. With disgust. And her last words to him still echoed in his mind.

You can't give me what I want, Max. A child. So I'm leaving you for someone who can.

He set his coffee cup down, shoved both hands into his pockets and rocked back on his heels. That was why he was so certain that Julia was lying to him about her pregnancy. He already knew he couldn't have children. He was infertile. He'd let go of his dreams of building a family empire.

There was a brief knock at his office door, then it opened, and his assistant, Tom Doheny, poked his head around the edge of it. "Mr. Rolland? There's a woman here to see you. A Ms. Prentice. She says it's urgent."

Max smiled and it couldn't have been a pleasant one since Tom's features tightened in response.

"Send her in."

Four

Once she'd explained everything, Julia stopped talking, turned around and faced Max. She hadn't been able to look at him while she told him about the blackmail letter. She couldn't force herself to face him and admit that she didn't have enough ready cash to pay the blackmailer what he/she wanted. And she really couldn't bring herself to do exactly what she'd gone to him to do in the first place.

Ask for help.

Now, as she stared across the massive office to where he sat perched on the edge of his desk, long legs stretched out in front of him, feet crossed at the ankles, she took a breath and waited. Seconds ticked past, measured by the hard thump of her heartbeat. Her mouth was dry, her stomach was in knots, and looking into Max's cool green eyes didn't make her feel any better.

When the silence stretched on, Julia broke first. "Well? Aren't you going to say anything?"

He folded his arms over his chest, cocked his head to one side and asked, "Why come to me with this?"

"Because it's *your* baby I'm carrying," she argued, and knew the moment she'd said the words it had been the wrong tack to take.

"Don't start that again," he said, lips so grimly compressed it was a wonder any words at all had escaped his mouth. "Let's stick with the facts, shall we?" He pushed away from the desk and started to prowl the room.

Julia's gaze fixed on him as he moved, his long legs making great strides, his footsteps soundless on the thick carpet. Diffused sunlight speared through the tinted windows, and the sounds of the city were so muted as to be nonexistent. It was as if she and Max were the only two people in the world.

How unfortunate that they weren't friends.

"The way I see it," he said, stalking the perimeter of the room, making her turn to keep him in sight, "you're pregnant and you don't want the world to know it just yet."

"True." Julia took a breath, held it for a second, then blew it out. "If this person makes good on his threat—" She broke off, unwilling to put into words the fears that had chased her since opening that damned envelope.

"You'll be fodder for the gossips for months."

"Years," she corrected darkly. "My child would hear the whispers and I can't let that happen."

"Eventually, you'll be faced with this problem, anyway," he pointed out.

"I'll think of something," she said, hoping to convince herself, as well as Max. "But I can't let this get out now. Not yet."

"And the reason you're not going to the father of this child?"

She glared at him. Did he honestly believe she was the kind of woman who would be pregnant with one man's child while telling another that *he* was the father? His features were twisted into a sardonic smile that let her know it was exactly what he thought. "He won't believe me," she said.

"Ahh. So I'm not the only man in your life with a low tolerance for lies."

She jerked as if he'd slapped her. What had she been thinking, coming to him? She'd deliberately walked into the lion's den, asked him to open his mouth, then set her head inside it so she could allow him to bite it off!

"You know what?" Julia muttered, turning for the door. "This was a mistake. I see that now. Just…never mind. Forget I was here."

He caught her before she could reach out and grab the doorknob. His grip on her upper arm was firm, unshakable. Still, she tried. When she failed, though, she lifted her gaze to his, gave him a glare that should have frozen him solid on the spot and said, "Let me go, Max."

"I don't think so." Instead, he turned her around, steered her to his desk and gave her a gentle shove into one of the leather chairs. "We're not through talking."

She tilted her head back to give him another dirty look. "Oh, I think we've said everything there is to say."

"Well, you're wrong," he told her, and sat down in the chair beside hers. Bracing both elbows on his knees, he locked his gaze with hers and said, "Bottom line it for me, Julia. Why'd you come to me?"

Her posture got even straighter, if possible. Her chin lifted and she gathered up what little dignity she had left and wrapped it around her as if it were an ermine cloak. "I don't have enough readily available cash to pay this person. I thought maybe you could loan it to me." When he didn't say anything to that, she hurriedly added, "I'll pay you whatever interest you think is fair and—"

"No."

She blinked at him. "That's it? Just 'no'?"

"Paying a blackmailer's never a good idea." He sat back in his chair, propped his right foot on his left knee and idly tapped his fingertips against the arm of the chair. "You think a million will satisfy this person? No. Once you pay, you'll be forced to keep paying."

"Oh, God." Perfect posture forgotten, Julia slumped into her own chair. How had this happened? Who was behind this and why? What had she ever done to make someone act so viciously? And what was she going to do?

"The way I see it," Max said softly, as if plotting out a response even as he spoke, "your only choice here is to make your secret not worth telling."

"Excuse me?" Julia looked at him. His green eyes were narrowed, his strong, hard jaw tight and his mouth hardly more than a grim line. This was not a man to take lightly. This was the face of the man who'd taken Wall Street by storm. A modern-day warrior who'd slain his would-be competitors by leaving their financial bodies littered in his wake.

This was Max Rolland.

The unstoppable force behind Rolland Enterprises.

And Julia had the distinct feeling she was about to find out firsthand what it was like to have Max the Marauder going into battle on her behalf.

"All you have to do is marry me."

Did he actually *say* those words?

She couldn't be sure. It was as if the whole world had suddenly stopped and tilted weirdly on its axis. If there was one thing she hadn't expected, it was a proposal.

"Are you— Did you— Why would you—" Not a good sign. She couldn't even string a complete sentence together.

He smiled at her and the smile was cold and calculating and didn't even approach his eyes. "Surprised?"

"Uh…yes," she admitted. "That would be a good way to put it."

"You shouldn't be." Standing up again, Max moved to the wet bar across the room, poured himself a cup of coffee and then asked, "You?"

"No, thanks."

"Right." He nodded to himself and smiled. "No caffeine for you. Don't know how you'll manage."

"I've got bigger things to worry about at the moment. And why should I have expected you to propose marriage to me? You don't even believe that this is your baby."

He took a sip of coffee, then walked back to where he'd left her. Looking down at her, he said, "No, I don't. But that's not the issue anymore."

She choked out a laugh. "What is?"

"You can't pay the blackmail. I *won't* pay it. I'm guessing you don't want your family to know about this pregnancy yet, either, am I right?"

More right than he knew. Julia got a cold chill just imagining breaking the "unwed mother" news to her parents. They'd once stopped speaking to her for six months because she'd dated a musician briefly.

The Prentices weren't exactly your average American family. She and her parents had never been close—which made one question why she cared what they thought of her life choices. But even if Margaret and Donald Prentice were cold and mostly uncaring, they were the only family Julia had. And now, more than ever, she couldn't afford to lose touch with that one fragile thread of connection.

"Yes," she whispered, ducking her head because she couldn't meet his eyes when she said it. "You're right."

"And the actual father of this child is no longer in the picture."

Wryly, she muttered, "You could say that."

"Seems to me, the one option open to you is marrying me. If we're married, then there is no scandal about your pregnancy. The blackmail will go away, end of problem."

"And beginning of another one," she countered, standing up now because tilting her head back to look at him simply put her at too great a disadvantage. "Max, I really appreciate your very unexpected offer of help, but don't you think it's going too far?"

"Why?" He set his coffee cup down on his desk, dropped both hands to her shoulders and held her gently, yet firmly. "We've got plenty of chemistry together, Julia. That's been proven."

"But a marriage?"

"Doesn't have to be forever," he qualified. "We can put a time stamp on it. Call it a marriage for a year. My attorney will draw up some papers and—"

"A year?"

"Less time would look suspicious, wouldn't it?"

"I suppose..." She felt as if she were being swept out to sea on a receding tidal wave. There was no ground beneath her feet. Nothing to grab hold of. Nowhere to turn. Nowhere to look but into his eyes. "But I still don't understand *why* you would do this."

"I want a son. An heir." He let her go, walked around the edge of his desk and stared out at the skyline of the great city sprawled out in front of them. "That's really all you need to know." Turning back to her, his gaze speared hers. "I'll marry you, give your child my name.

He'll be mine, legally and emotionally. You'll sign legal papers asserting that fact."

"And if the baby's a girl?"

He looked startled—as if he hadn't considered that possibility at all. Then he brushed the notion aside. "Doesn't matter. Girl or boy, the baby's mine the minute we get married. Agreed?"

No problem, she thought but didn't say. The baby *was* his, despite what he thought, so she wouldn't have any issues signing whatever documents he required. But there remained another question. "If we get married and want it to look real, we'll have to live together."

"Naturally."

"As husband and wife."

"Absolutely." He came back to her, his gaze never leaving her face.

Julia felt heat start at the top of her head and slide all the way down to the soles of her feet. His gaze swept her up and down as surely as a touch, and just like that, Julia's body slipped into overdrive.

When he touched her, she half expected to burst into flames. But all that happened was more heat, seeping from his hands on her shoulders down deep into her flesh.

"You'll move into my place. My bed. As far as anyone else knows, this is a whirlwind romance."

"Whirlwind…" She smiled in spite of everything. "Sounds appropriate."

"And when we're married," he said softly, "I'll expect you to tell me who the baby's father really is.

I'll want to know who to watch out for. Who to guard against."

"Max—"

He kissed her and Julia's mind simply shut down. There was no room for thinking when sensation was spilling through her like a river of molten lava. Every cell in her body was alive and awake and clamoring for more.

Max's hands swept up and down her spine, molding her body to his, pulling her in so tightly to him that Julia thought wildly for a moment that her body was going to slide right into his. Her arms came up and linked behind his neck, holding his head to hers, his mouth to hers. He parted her lips with his tongue and she lost her breath on a ragged sigh of pleasure so deep, so soul searingly complete, she gave herself up to the wonder of it.

All of this happened even while a small, still-rational corner of her mind explored this new situation. Marrying Max? Was she asking for more trouble? Was she blindly walking into a situation that was only going to lead to misery? Was she setting herself up to be broken and hurt?

Did she have a choice?

Max broke the kiss. He didn't let her go, just lifted his head and looked down at her. "Well? What's it going to be, Julia? Do we get married?"

Her head still reeling, her body whimpering, Julia looked up into those grass-green eyes. She saw the future stretching out unknown in front of them and knew that he was the best choice for her and her child. She didn't really *want* to marry a man who thought her capable of lying to him about something so personal, so important. But if she didn't marry Max and the blackmailer made good on his/her threat, then she and her child would be the subject of vicious gossip for years. Besides, it wasn't as if she was marrying a stranger. He was the father of her child.

This was her best…her *only* real choice. So she would marry Max. And somehow, she would find a way to convince him that the child she carried was his. With that thought firmly in mind, she heard herself say, "Yes, Max. We get married."

"Excellent."

Then he kissed her again and the deal was sealed.

"A prenup? You're getting married? When did this happen?"

Max looked across the table at his attorney and friend, Alexander Harper. Tall, with dark hair and dark eyes, Alex looked dangerous, which Max appreciated in an attorney.

"It's a sudden decision," Max allowed, taking a sip of the fifty-year-old scotch in front of him.

"Damn sudden if you ask me," Alex said, lifting a hand to signal the waitress for a scotch like his friend. He'd arrived a little late for their business lunch and had some catching up to do. "Aren't you the guy who swore he'd never get married again after what happened with Camille?"

Frowning a little, Max nodded. "This is different." In a few short sentences, he laid it all out for his friend, who shook his head and thanked their waitress for his drink when it arrived. Lifting the heavy crystal tumbler, he took a sip, set the glass down again and said, "That's a hell of a thing, Max. And Julia Prentice is quite the catch."

Max knew that. Hell, Julia's bloodlines were better than Camille's. The Prentice family was old money. They'd been around forever and guarded their name with the tenacity of a pen of pit bulls. Wryly, he admitted silently that he'd love to see the faces of Julia's parents when she broke it to them that she'd be marrying him. A self-made billionaire, son of a truck driver and a housewife.

His gaze swept the interior of the small, upscale restaurant. Only a dozen or so tables filled the wood-paneled room, and those tables were covered in snowy-white linen. Waiters wearing black slacks and crisp white shirts moved through the room with silent efficiency. The darkly tinted windows looked out on Fifth Avenue, and for a moment, Max distracted himself by staring at the crowds of people streaming along the sidewalks.

"So," Alex said, drawing his attention back to the conversation at hand, "you don't believe her about the baby, but you're marrying her, anyway."

"That's about the size of it. I need you to draw up a prenup and also a document stating I'm the father of her child." The more he'd thought about this situation in the hour or so since Julia had left his office, the more Max liked the situation. He was getting a bed partner who lit his sheets on fire, and he was getting the child he so badly wanted. It was a win-win as far as he could see. And knowing going in that the woman he was about to marry was a beautiful liar gave him the advantage. Again. "I want it signed, notarized…hell, I want it bronzed, before the ceremony."

"All doable," Alex said, then pinned his friend with a hard look. "But tell me something. Why are you so fast to discount the possibility that you are the baby's father?"

Frowning again, Max said, "You know why."

"Yeah, Camille told you the tests came back saying you were infertile."

Max scowled at him. Alex had never been a fan of Camille's. Even knowing that his friend had been right didn't change things. "I *saw* the damn test results."

"You saw what Camille wanted you to see."

They'd been over this before and Max was tired of the trip. So he cut his friend off at the pass. "Look, I don't want to talk about ancient history. I just need you to take care of these details, all right?"

"Sure, Max," Alex said with a shrug. "I'll take care of it. How soon do you need it done?"

"The wedding's in two weeks."

Alex whistled, low and long. "I'll have to hustle to get it all set up."

"Well, my friend," Max said with a self-satisfied smile, "that's why you make the big bucks, isn't it?

Now, let's eat. I'm picking Julia up in an hour to go see the police."

"At least that much makes sense to me," Alex said, picking up his leather-bound menu to peruse it. "Who're you going to be talking to? Do you have a name?"

"A Detective McGray," Max said, sliding his gaze over the restaurant's offerings. "He's in charge of the investigation into the death of the woman who lived in Julia's building. I figured, the blackmail's in the building, too. Might as well see the man who's already investigating what's happening at 721."

Detective Arnold McGray looked tired.

His salt-and-pepper hair stood on end and his eyes had dark shadows beneath them. A five-o'clock shadow stubbled his jaws, and his dark blue tie had been loosened at his undone collar.

"Let me see if I have this straight," he said, glancing down at the notepad he'd been writing on since Julia had started talking. "You're being blackmailed and you have no idea who might be behind this?"

"That's right." Julia stiffened, instinctively uncomfortable in the bustling detective area of the local NYPD precinct building.

Around her, overworked and underpaid police officers were hunkered down over desks littered with manila file folders, towering stacks of papers and ringing phones. The cacophony was deafening. A drunken homeless man was singing to himself, a hooker in a bright red dress was trying to proposition her way out of an arrest, and a bearded younger man rattled the handcuffs that kept him locked in his chair.

This was so far out of Julia's everyday world, she didn't know where to look.

"And you think this might have something to do with the death of Marie Endicott?" McGray's voice was pitched just loud enough to carry over the noise.

"What?" Julia shook herself and frowned. "No, I mean, I don't know. It's possible, I suppose…" She glanced at Max, sitting beside her.

Even in this setting, his personal stamp of power was easy to read. He didn't look intimidated or threatened by the surroundings. Clearly, he was a man completely at home and confident of himself wherever he was.

As if picking up on her uncertainty, Max took the thread of her conversation and finished it himself. "Detective McGray," he said, "the truth is, my fiancée and I have no idea who might be behind this blackmail attempt. My feeling was that we should bring the matter to you, as it could very well be part of what's happened at my fiancée's building."

Julia had to force herself not to jerk in reaction to the word *fiancée*. He'd used it twice, as if making a point either to her or the detective. Which? she wondered, and then asked herself if it mattered.

She'd already agreed to marry him. And though a part of her was worried about what would happen, another, more cowardly part was grateful for the reprieve Max had offered her. The fact that the child she carried actually *was* his, was, she thought, ironic.

"I appreciate you bringing the matter to my attention," McGray said, slumping back in his tattered chair. "Frankly, I wouldn't be surprised if there was a connection."

"Really?" Julia asked.

"Seems unlikely that two such unrelated events would happen in the span of a couple of weeks—in a place that's seen no trouble at all in more than ten years."

"My thoughts exactly," Max said, reaching out to give Julia's cold hand a squeeze.

"Well, I've got all I need for the moment," the detective said, standing up behind his desk. "I'll look into this and if I find anything, I'll be in touch."

Max stood up, too, and held out one hand. When the older man shook it, Max thanked him. Then almost before she knew what was happening, Julia found herself being steered out of the police precinct and led outside.

"Do you really think the blackmailer has something to do with what happened to Marie Endicott?" Julia asked when they were alone.

He glanced over her head at the teeming streets, then led her down the steps to the sidewalk. Lifting one hand to hail a cab, Max glanced down at her. "My gut says yeah. They're related."

"Then that means…"

"We're not sure what it means," he cautioned, his

green eyes going cold and hard. "But yes, your black-mailer could have been involved in that woman's death."

"Oh, God." Julia hadn't wanted to think of Marie committing suicide. But the thought of a murderer walking free through 721 Park Avenue was even more disquieting.

A chill swept over her, making her shiver despite the cloying heat and humidity pounding down on the city.

Five

Max stared up at the edifice of 721 Park Avenue, craning his neck to take in the entire fourteen-story brick facade. A prewar structure, 721 was a classic in the old style. The building settled into the corner of Park and Seventieth like an old woman in a comfortable chair.

The city itself had grown and changed over the years, but the old building remained the same, sitting in the heart of the most expensive slice of real estate in the United States. Politicians, celebrities, old money and new, all gravitated to the Upper East Side of New York. And this place was one of the crown jewels of the neighborhood.

All around him, the city pulsed with life and

energy. People streamed past him on the sidewalk, and on the streets car horns blasted out a cacophony of sound.

Max ignored it all, though, as his gaze fixed on the roof and his thoughts turned to the woman who'd fallen to her death from that very roof. Then he thought about the blackmail attempt on Julia and asked himself, just what the hell was going on at 721? He agreed with the police detective they'd spoken to the day before. It seemed highly unlikely that two such-out-of-the-normal events could happen within a couple of weeks of each other and not be related somehow.

Lowering his gaze to the glass door that opened into the quietly elegant lobby of the building, Max spied the doorman wandering over to his desk. Smiling to himself, Max stepped up, pulled open the front door and stepped into the cool quiet of the lobby. Vastly different from his own building's entry, 721 reeked of old-world elegance and a time long past.

Instantly the doorman's gaze snapped up to meet Max's. "Good afternoon," he said. "May I help you?"

Max walked up to the impressive mahogany desk behind which the much smaller man stood. Taking a quick look around the lobby area, Max spotted the mailboxes for the tenants and smiled to himself. Just as he'd thought. The doorman would have had a good view of whoever might have slipped a blackmail letter into Julia's mail slot.

Rather than answering the man's question, Max gave him a tight smile and said, "You're Henry, right?"

The doorman looked surprised. "Yes, sir. Henry Brown."

"My fiancée lives in this building," Max said, and realized that it was getting easier to say the word fiancée. "Ms. Prentice."

There was a flicker of surprise in Henry's dark brown eyes, which disappeared a moment later. "Are you here to see her, then? She's not at home at the moment, but I'd be happy to deliver a message for you."

Trying to get rid of him? Max wondered. "No," he said, "actually, I came to talk to you."

"Me?"

Max had made it a point over the years to learn how to read people. It came in handy in negotiations and was invaluable when meeting new clients or prospective business partners. And every instinct Max had told him that Henry was nervous. It didn't show clearly, of course, and if he hadn't been looking for the signals, he might have missed them himself.

But Henry's gaze was furtive, darting around the lobby as if looking for help that wasn't going to come. His right hand was fisted on his desk and the fingers of his left hand tapped restlessly against a pad of paper with 721 in elegant script across the top.

Interesting, Max thought and smiled inwardly. "Yes, Henry. I want you to think back on the last few days."

"About what?"

"Have you seen anyone in here who didn't belong?" Max leaned one arm on the desktop. "Anyone who might have dropped an envelope into one of the mailboxes?"

Henry blinked as if he was stepping out of the shadows and into the light. His mouth opened and closed a couple of times, then he swallowed hard and shook his head. "No, sir, I haven't. And nothing like that would happen without me seeing it. I'm on duty right here. No one would get in who didn't belong."

"I did," Max pointed out.

Henry licked his upper lip, blew out a breath and said, "What I meant was, no one could stay inside who didn't talk to me first. And no one but the mailman and the residents go near the mailboxes."

"You're sure about that?"

Henry lifted his narrow chin, met Max's gaze with the direct stare of an honest man and said, "Absolutely."

Max was sure about something, too.

Henry was lying.

Max couldn't prove it, but he knew it down to his bones. And that made him wonder what exactly was going on at 721. The old place looked quiet, dignified. But there were undercurrents here and Max didn't like it. He didn't want to think about Julia staying here. One woman was dead and Julia herself was being blackmailed.

Something was very wrong in this building.

"You're pregnant?"

Julia winced as her mother's voice hit a particularly high note. She'd known this was going to be an ugly meeting. She had to face her parents not only with the news of her pregnancy, but her upcoming marriage, as well.

She sighed a little as her mother stood up from her silk-brocade chair and stared down at Julia as though she were a particularly appalling bug. *Just imagine,* she thought, *what this scene would have been like if you hadn't been able to tell them you're getting married.*

The sting of their only daughter being an unwed mother was something her parents might never have recovered from. All her life, Julia had been a disappointment. She knew that. Her parents had made sure of it. And all of her life, a part of Julia had tried to make them proud. To make them love her. Despite her efforts, nothing had changed.

She looked up at her mother and felt…nothing. No connection. No bond. No threads of affection or familial loyalty. Just…nothing. As sad as that made her, Julia realized that accepting this was the first step in finding her own kind of peace. The first step in building her own family. Her own world, separate and apart from the people who'd made her.

"Yes," Julia said, smiling into her mother's disapproving gaze, "I am. And my baby's father and I will be getting married in just a couple of weeks."

"That's something, I suppose," her father muttered from the chair where he sat glaring at her. "As long as you're married quickly, no one will have to know the reason."

Julia glanced at him and noticed that his bushy gray eyebrows were drawn together in a too-familiar frown of disgust. She couldn't remember a single time in her life when her father had held her, hugged her, told her that she was pretty or that he loved her. How strange it was to sit here in this place and realize the sad truth of her life.

She didn't have a family. She had biological parents. That was all.

And because she knew that they would never approve of her or give her the kind of love she'd once longed for, Julia was free. Free to speak her mind. To tell them what she'd feared telling them only days before.

Straightening in her chair, she clasped her fingers together tightly in her lap and said, "People will know I'm going to have a baby, Father."

"Eventually," he conceded with a shake of his head.

"Donald, you're missing the point here," Margaret Prentice snapped. "This will make us *grandparents*. For heaven's sake, I don't want people thinking I'm old enough to be a grandmother. This is a disaster."

"Thank you," Julia muttered.

"You will not speak to us in such a fashion, Julia," her mother said as her cold blue gaze fixed on her daughter. "At the very least, you owe us civility and respect."

"Respect is a two-way street, Mother."

Margaret laughed shortly. "Respect? You expect us to respect you for being stupid enough to get pregnant? You ask too much."

"Having a baby isn't stupid," Julia argued.

"You're not even married," her father said.

"I will be soon," she responded, feeling a fire begin

to build inside her. For years, when there were "discussions" like this one, she'd kept her mouth shut, done what was expected of her. But not anymore. She owed her child more than that. She owed *herself* more than that.

"How could you do this to me?" Margaret's voice shrieked a little.

"I didn't *do* anything to you, Mother…"

"None of my friends are grandmothers," her mother said hotly. "How will this look to people? How can I face my friends?" She crossed her too-thin arms over her narrow chest, but not tightly enough to wrinkle the cream-colored silk blouse she wore tucked into the waistband of linen pants the color of wheat. Margaret's elegantly styled hair was short and dyed honey-blond every four weeks. Her manicure was perfect, her make-up expertly applied, and her unlined face was a billboard for the best cosmetic surgeons in the city.

"Mother—"

"Don't speak to me."

"If we keep the ceremony quiet," Donald Prentice mused more to himself than anyone else, "it's possible—"

"What?" Margaret turned on her husband like a cobra. "That no one will notice when Julia's body begins to swell? People will notice, I assure you. And my friends will never let me forget that I'm a *grand-mother,* for pity's sake."

It was as if Julia wasn't even present. They talked around her, over her, about her, as if she wasn't their daughter at all, but some annoying distant relative who'd made a claim on them they didn't care to acknowledge.

This she was used to. She'd grown accustomed to being nothing more than an annoyance to the people who should have loved her the most. Her succession of nannies had given her the only affection she'd known in her childhood, and as she grew older, Julia had realized that her parents had never wanted children in the first place.

At fifteen, she'd actually heard her mother telling a friend one day about "accidentally" getting pregnant and what a horror it had been. Julia glanced around the living room of the home where she'd grown up and realized that she'd never once felt comfortable there. Never once had she felt as though she belonged.

And that still held true. The walls were a glaring white with only a few abstract paintings lending garish splotches of color to the cold room. The floors were white tile and the chairs and couches, upholstered in subtle, differing shades of beige, were designed more for appearance than comfort. Even the smell of the house was sterile, as if the air in the place had long since died and was only being recycled by the people who continued to breathe it.

Rubbing at her temples, Margaret glared at Julia. "Who, may I inquire, is the father of this unfortunate child?"

Julia squirmed in her chair and cupped one hand over her still-flat abdomen as if she could prevent her baby from hearing its grandparents' dismissal of its very existence. "His name is Max. Max Rolland."

Margaret frowned, though her too-tight forehead prevented it from showing. "Rolland. Hmm. No, I don't believe I know any Rollands. Donald?"

Julia waited, knowing that this news would completely wipe away her parents' fury at hearing about the baby. Discovering that their only child was about to marry a man with no pedigree would put everything else they'd heard into perspective for them.

Strangely enough, Julia was almost looking forward to their reaction.

"Max Rolland…" Her father repeated the name thoughtfully.

"Who are his people?" Margaret demanded.

"His parents have passed away," Julia told her.

"I didn't ask *where* they were," Margaret reminded her, "I said *who* are they?"

"I know the name Rolland," her father said from his chair. "I just can't place it."

"Max is from upstate," Julia told her mother. Then, smiling, she took a breath and added, "His father was, I believe, a truck driver and his mother was a housewife."

Margaret slapped one hand to her chest and staggered backward as if someone had shoved a sword through her body.

"Rolland!" Donald Prentice shouted the name and pounded one fist against the arm of his chair. "That's how I know the name. That upstart running roughshod over Wall Street. He's made something of a name for himself, but—"

"A *truck driver?*" Margaret moaned softly, dropped back into her chair and lifted one hand to cover her eyes. "Oh, dear God, how did this happen?"

Julia paid no attention to the drama. "Max is very successful," she said. "He's a…good man." That might have been a bit of a stretch, she told herself, but at the same time, she realized that only a good man would have proposed to help her out. Whether he saw it that way or not, if he'd been a different sort of man, he'd have left her to solve her own problem or drown in her own misery.

"A *housewife?*" Margaret whispered the word as if afraid someone might hear her.

"People say he's cold and ruthless," Donald was saying, though his wife wasn't listening and Julia didn't want to hear him. "Could be quite a force in the city if he had a family name behind him."

"He's doing just fine without a 'name,'" Julia argued.

"No doubt," Donald said with a frown. "But there are limits to what a man like him can accomplish."

"Because his blood isn't blue?" Julia stood up and looked at her parents each in turn. "That's ridiculous. Max Rolland is a good, hardworking man who made his own fortune rather than inherited it."

"Exactly," Donald said with a slow shake of his head.

Sunlight streamed through the windows, glancing off the white walls and floors until Julia's eyes stung with the cold, hard brilliance of it all. Why had she been so concerned with telling her parents about her baby? Why had she been so terrified that she might lose this one slender thread of family?

The truth was, she'd never had a family to lose. She'd always been alone.

Until now, anyway.

Now she had her baby.

And she had Max.

"You can't possibly be serious about marrying this person." Her mother posed it as a sentence, not a question.

"I'm more serious about it with every passing second," Julia assured her, picking up her purse and slipping the slim leather strap over her shoulder.

"Julia, don't do something you'll regret," her father warned.

"I've already done that, Father," Julia told him as she turned to leave. "I came here expecting support. I'm not sure why, exactly, but this visit is definitely something I regret."

She walked briskly across the room, through the doorway and down the stairs where a maid in uniform waited to open the front door for her. Julia reached the bottom of the steps and turned when her mother called her name sharply.

Margaret Prentice stood at the head of the stairs, looking as cool and unapproachable as a queen. "What is it, Mother?"

"Don't think for one moment, young woman, that your father and I will acknowledge your marriage to this man. If you do this, you turn your back on your family."

A small twist of fear became a knot in the pit of her stomach, but then, as she drew one long breath, that knot dissolved. Strange, Julia thought, that it was at the moment her life was most in turmoil that she should find such an incredible sense of peace.

"I understand, Mother. Goodbye."

The door closed firmly behind her.

By the following day, Julia was too busy to spend much time worrying about her parents. She had a wedding to plan and a move to organize.

"It's going to be great," Amanda said as they settled into a couple of armchairs at the Park Café. Reaching into her leather briefcase, Amanda pulled out a thick day planner and quickly scanned her notes. "I know Max wants a fast wedding," she said with a wink for Julia, "but that doesn't mean it can't be fabulous. I've got the names of some caterers and I'd like you to look at some samples from the florist I've been working with."

Julia had notes of her own to check and they didn't have anything to do with her upcoming wedding. She was in the middle of a fund-raiser for a Manhattan shelter, and there were still one or two things that had to be nailed down. "Why don't you pick the caterer, Amanda? I swear I haven't had enough of an appetite to even *think* about food lately."

Her friend frowned a bit, reached for her ice blended

mocha and took a sip. Her gaze fixed on Julia until she squirmed uncomfortably.

"You haven't been feeling well ever since you went to see your folks," Amanda said.

"Can you blame me?" Julia forced a smile and told herself she'd be fine. She'd be *great*. She had her work, she had her baby and soon she'd have her very own husband, complete with prenup, baby contract and suspicion.

"No," Amanda said, "who can blame you? I'm just saying, the wedding's coming and you really should pay attention."

Julia closed her folder, sighed and leaned back into her chair. The café was crowded at lunchtime, and the noise level was such that Julia felt safe enough talking about what was really bothering her. "It's not the wedding or my parents," she said, leaning in a bit closer. "It's the fact that I'm moving in with Max in a few days."

Amanda laughed. "Honey, you're marrying him."

"I know, I know." Julia frowned and told herself she was being foolish. "But living with him is a little…"

"Exciting?"

"I was going to go with 'unnerving.'"

"Why?"

"Because of the way we're getting married," she said. "And the fact that he still doesn't believe me about the baby."

"Well, he's an idiot. We already decided that." Amanda went back to her lists.

"I know, but how'm I supposed to convince him that he is the father?"

"You may not be able to until the baby's born. Then you can do a paternity test."

"So that leaves me with seven months of my husband thinking I'm a liar."

Amanda closed her folder, picked up her mocha and idly twirled the straw through the thick, pale brown liquid. "You know I'm with you, no matter what, right?"

"Of course."

She smiled. "And you know I'm completely excited that you're letting me take over your apartment when you move in with Max…"

"I know."

"But," Amanda said, leaning forward to pat Julia's hand, "if you're really worried about this, don't do it."

"What?" Julia glanced across the room when someone laughed too loudly. Then, looking back at Amanda, she said, "I have to."

"No, you don't. You've already faced the worst part. You've told your parents."

"And the blackmail?" Julia shook her head slowly, despite being grateful for what Amanda was trying to tell her. God knew, after the afternoon with her parents, Julia was even more thankful to have Amanda's unswerving support. But the simple truth was, she had to marry Max. Otherwise, her child would be the subject of vicious gossip before it was even born. And she wouldn't allow that. "I appreciate it, sweetie," Julia said. "But I have to marry Max."

"Getting married for the wrong reasons is so not a good idea," Amanda said softly.

"Marriage for *any* reason isn't usually a good idea." A deep voice resonated from just behind Julia and she swiveled to look up at the man staring down at her.

"Hello, Max."

Six

"Okay," Amanda said, grabbing her drink and standing up in one smooth move. "That's my cue to hit the road."

"You don't have to go on my account," Max said, already dropping onto the couch beside Julia.

"No, it's okay. I've got lots of calls to make," Amanda told him, then shifted her gaze to Julia's. "We'll talk later at home, okay?"

"Sure, see you later." Julia watched her friend leave, then turned her head to look at Max, who was studying her carefully.

"Your friend trying to talk you out of this?"

"She's worried about me."

"Should she be?" He ran the tips of his fingers down

the length of her arm, and even through her linen shirt Julia felt heat, a heat that began to slide through her veins.

"Good question," she said, and shifted slightly, drawing her arm back and away from him. How could she think when he was touching her?

"Is there an answer?" He eased back, the sides of his black suit jacket falling to either side of him, displaying what she knew to be a rock-solid chest and abdomen hidden beneath the custom-made dress shirt.

She lifted her gaze to his and blew out a breath. "I don't know. Max, Amanda's my friend. She's trying to be supportive, letting me know she's on my side no matter what."

"She knows what's going on?" he asked. "The baby? The blackmail?"

"Yes." Julia glanced around the coffee shop, checking to see who was watching them. Who might be listening. She knew darn well that whoever was behind the blackmail had to have overheard her and Max talking about the baby in here. When she looked back to him, though, she let the worry go. The blackmail had already happened. What more could this person do to her? "I told her everything."

"Including the name of the father of your baby?" he wondered aloud, his gaze narrowing slightly.

"Max…" Irritation spiked inside her and Julia fought the distinct urge to kick him in the shins. Honestly. She'd lived her whole life by the rules. She'd maintained the sophisticated facade that life in society demanded. She'd never stepped out of line, always done just what she should.

And the minute she met Max, all that had disappeared. Not only had she slept with him right away, she'd gotten pregnant. Not only was she being blackmailed, she was marrying a man she hardly knew. Not only was he the father of her child, but she couldn't make him believe she wasn't a liar. And now, the well-behaved, always discreet Julia Prentice wanted to kick a man and scream at him in public, and the only thing keeping her from doing just that was what was left of her self-control.

"Wow," he mused aloud, a barely concealed chuckle in his tone, "you just had quite the talk with yourself, didn't you?"

"What?"

He sat up, braced his elbows on his knees and locked his gaze with hers. "Your face. It's so easy to read, it's ridiculous. You don't keep secrets well, do you."

"No, I really don't," she muttered, disturbed a little at how easily he could read her. But then she told herself it didn't matter, since even reading her face so expertly, he didn't believe what he saw. "I'm not a good liar, Max. That's why I don't lie."

"Uh-huh." Max would have liked to believe her, but how could he? Those big blue eyes of hers seemed to look right through him, and he wondered what she saw in him. What she'd seen from the beginning that had sent her to him for help when her world had crashed down around her.

He glanced around the café and reassured himself no one was paying the slightest attention to the two of them. Turning back to Julia, he watched her squirm uncomfortably on the couch and read her body language easily enough. She was uneasy in his presence and he thought he knew why.

"You went to see your parents yesterday, didn't you?"

Her eyes darkened a bit in memory, and Max knew he'd guessed right. He was willing to bet that the elder Prentices hadn't been happy with their daughter's news.

"Yes."

"Told them about the baby?"

"Yes." She shifted, tugged the hem of her pale blue skirt closer to her knees and crossed her feet daintily at the ankle. As neatly as a nun, she folded her hands together in her lap. "They were…unhappy."

He laughed shortly. "I'm guessing that's an understatement."

She winced. "Pretty much."

Max didn't need her to explain what that conversation had been like. He'd met her parents briefly at some social function in the city and hadn't exactly been impressed with their warmth. In fact, he found it amazing that a woman with the fire Julia had could have come from people so inherently cold.

Oddly enough, looking at her now, seeing the distress that still clouded her eyes at the mention of her parents, Max realized that he'd like nothing better than to go see them. Tell them what he thought of parents who couldn't bring themselves to support their own child.

"My mother," Julia said, capturing his attention, "is appalled at the idea of being labeled a grandmother."

"Her loss," he said tightly, and was rewarded by a flash of light in her eyes. Wanting to see that spark again, he said, "My mother would have been on cloud nine."

"Really?"

Max smiled. He didn't often think of his parents, because memories only made him miss them more. But now he allowed his mother's smiling image to fill his mind. "Oh, yeah. She used to harp on me all the time about making her a grandmother. She'd have been excited at the prospect."

Julia's mouth curved gently, sadly. "I'm sorry she's not here to know you're going to be a father."

Instantly his insides tightened. "We both know that's not true, though, don't we?"

"Max, please believe me," she said, reaching out one hand to him. Her fingers closed around his and in response, he felt heat shoot up the length of his arm and slam into his chest.

And because that sensation was so strong, he battled it back, refusing to be swayed by it. Instead, he squeezed her fingers briefly, then let go. "What'd your folks have to say about the wedding?"

She sighed, clearly understanding that he wanted a change in subject. "Well, that news took their minds off the baby."

This time, Max's laugh boomed out into the café and several heads turned to look. Ignoring them, he straightened, leaned in closer to her and said, "Not surprising, is it? The fact that I could buy and sell your father three times over isn't enough to make up for the lack of a pedigree?"

"Not to them."

"But you don't care?" He watched her. He'd know if she lied in her response, and suddenly, he really wanted to know what she thought. He knew she was only marrying him because she felt she had no choice. But he needed to know what she thought of him. What she really felt.

"Of course I don't," she said, and he knew instinctively that it was the truth. A glint of anger shone briefly in her eyes as she fixed her gaze on him. "Do you really think I'm that shallow? Do I strike you as someone who cares more about a person's background than the person himself?"

He studied her for a long moment, taking in the heightened color in her cheeks and the light of battle in her eyes. "No," he said finally, his voice low and soft, "you don't."

"Well, that's something, anyway," Julia muttered. "You still think I'm a liar, but at least you don't believe I'm elitist about it."

He gave her a quick grin. "See? We're already getting along great."

Julia frowned at him.

"They really gave you a bad time, didn't they?" he asked, his smile fading.

"No more than I was expecting."

"I'm sorry it was hard on you," he said, reacting more to the glimmer of pain in her eyes than to anything else.

"Are you?" she asked.

"Of course I am. I'd feel sorry for anyone who'd had to grow up with those two polar bears."

She stiffened a little and Max admired her instinctive defensive posture. Even though she and her parents weren't close, it was apparent she wasn't going to let anyone else speak badly of them.

"They're not bad people," she said, and he wondered if she was trying to convince him or herself. "They just never should have had children."

Again he studied her for a long minute, then said quietly, "I'm glad they did."

"Really?" She shook her head and gave him a wry smile. "Why would you be glad? You're marrying a woman you don't love and agreeing to be the father of a child you don't believe you created."

"I'm marrying my lover," he said, lowering his voice until it was nothing more than a low rumble of sound pitched so only she could hear him. "A woman who sets my body on fire with a glance. And I'm getting the heir I want. Like I said before, a win-win for me."

"I don't understand you," she said, tipping her head to one side as if trying to get a better picture of the man. "You're taking this so lightly."

"No, I'm not," Max assured her, leaning in so close that he felt her breath on his face. "Trust me when I say I'm taking this very seriously."

"What if we're miserable together?"

"We won't be."

"How do you know?" Her gaze locked with his.

"I'll just keep you in bed as much as I can. We've already proven we get along just fine there."

"There's more to a marriage than sex."

"Sure," he quipped. "There's children, too. And we've already got that taken care of."

"Max—"

"Stop trying to make this harder than it has to be," Max said firmly. He wasn't going to let her change her mind. Wasn't going to allow her nerves to stretch to the point where she simply snapped and called everything off.

He'd gone into this with his eyes open, knowing he could help her and himself. And now that they'd reached an agreement, Max could admit that he wanted this marriage. He wanted her in his house. In his bed. There was no way he would let her wriggle out of their bargain.

"I'm not," she argued. "I guess I just need to know that we're doing the right thing."

"Do you have the money for the blackmailer?" he asked flatly.

"No."

"Do you want to tell your parents that the wedding's off, but the baby's still on?"

"No," she said and slumped back into her seat.

"Then we're doing the right thing."

"I wonder," she said, "is the *only* thing necessarily the *right* thing?"

"You're thinking too much," he said. "Decision's been made. Let it go."

Her gaze locked on his and her expression was even easier to read than usual. Stubborn resignation. Good. At least she was accepting that this wedding *was* going to happen.

"Look," Max said abruptly. "I was on my way to a meeting when I walked past the café and saw you sitting in here with Amanda. I only came in to tell you something." He wasn't going to let her know that it had been a spur-of-the-moment decision. That seeing her had hit him so hard he hadn't been able to resist coming in to talk to her.

"Fine, then. What is it?"

"My lawyer says he'll have the papers ready for us to sign tomorrow morning."

"So soon?" She looked a little nervous, and a part of Max was glad to see it. Those few nerves told him that she wasn't a cold, calculating woman—as if he needed to be convinced. She might be lying to him, but he was willing to bet she hadn't set any of this in motion on purpose.

Max checked his watch again, then met her gaze. "I'll pick you up at nine. We can take care of the paperwork and be finished before the movers show up at your place."

"Oh, I didn't hire movers yet."

"It's already arranged," Max said. "They'll be at your place to pack by eleven tomorrow."

"Tomorrow?" Julia stared at him. "That's too soon.

I'm not ready, and besides, don't you think I can handle this myself? I don't need you to step in and—"

He leaned in and kissed her hard and quick, instantly cutting off her arguments. "No need to thank me," he said, giving her a grin that let her know he was completely aware of her frustration.

"Max…"

"I've got that meeting. I'll see you in the morning." Then he stood up and walked out, never looking back. Not that he had to. He felt her gaze boring a hole in his back.

Impatient, Julia tapped the toe of her shoe against the cold, marble floor of her lobby while she waited for the ancient elevator to arrive. Irritation with Max's high-handedness still stung.

"I can take care of myself," she muttered darkly. "Been doing it for years without any help, thanks very much."

Then she winced and glanced over her shoulder to make sure the doorman hadn't heard her. But Henry was oblivious to her presence, chatting away on the telephone at his desk. Good. She didn't need one more male sticking his nose into her business.

Honestly, did Max really think he could simply arrange her life to suit him? If he did, this temporary marriage was going to get off to a rocky start. She glanced up at the old-fashioned dial on the elevator and saw that it was going up, not coming down. Apparently someone in one of the penthouses had called for it.

Sighing, Julia turned, crossed the lobby and headed for the residents' mailboxes. Might as well pick up the mail now since she had a few minutes.

"Ms. Prentice!" Henry called.

Inserting the key into her box, Julia opened it, took out the stack of envelopes and mailers, then closed and relocked it before answering. "Yes?"

Sunlight slanted through the glass door and lay in a wide swath on the marble. Henry walked right through the light and stopped a couple of feet from her. "I wanted to tell you, like I told your fiancé…"

Fiancé, she thought, and wondered if she would be used to the sound of that word before she had to become accustomed to the word *husband*.

"Max? You talked to Max?"

"Yes, ma'am," Henry said, and bobbed his head nervously. But then, Henry always looked nervous and a little too cowed by the residents of the building. "He asked if I'd seen anyone hanging around the mailboxes and I told him I hadn't."

Julia glanced at the mailboxes and tightened her grip on the envelopes she held. Max had thought to question Henry. She hadn't and she should have, darn it. But in her own defense, she'd been a little too upset by the whole blackmail thing to sit down and rationally investigate it. Still, now that the thought was in her mind…

"Are you sure, Henry?" she asked, staring directly into his eyes until he shifted his gaze from hers. "It wouldn't have taken long for someone to drop a letter into one of the boxes."

He shrugged and when the phone at his desk rang, he jumped as if he'd been shot. "I'm sure. It's my job to watch over this lobby."

"Yes," she was saying, but Henry had already turned away, headed back for the phone like a drowning man reaching for a life preserver. "But—"

"721 Park Avenue," Henry said, cutting her off neatly and devoting himself entirely to whoever was calling.

He kept his back to her and it was obvious to Julia that he had no intention of getting off the phone until she was on the elevator. For whatever reason, Henry didn't want to talk anymore about what had happened. That didn't necessarily make him guilty of anything, though, she reminded herself. All it did was underscore just what a nervous type the poor guy really was, and increase the tiny seed of suspicion about him that Max had planted.

Shaking her head, Julia headed back across the lobby, the sound of her heels clicking musically against the floor. The elevator dinged as she approached, the doors slid open and Elizabeth Wellington stepped out and stopped dead.

"Julia," she said, flashing a smile that wasn't deep enough to display the dimples in her cheeks.

Instantly, Julia felt a wash of sympathy for her friend. Up until a year or so ago, Elizabeth had been happy and bubbly. Now her green eyes looked sad and her red hair was mussed as if she'd been distractedly running her fingers through it.

"The grapevine in the building works incredibly well," Elizabeth was saying as she gave Julia another wan smile. "I hear congratulations are in order. Both for your engagement and your baby."

Julia nearly winced. Now she felt not only sympathy but almost a twinge of guilt, too. She'd been so worried about her unplanned pregnancy, and poor Elizabeth was miserable, dealing with her infertility issues.

"Thank you," Julia said, and meant it sincerely. She guessed what it cost Elizabeth to be happy for someone else when she so badly wanted a child of her own. Reaching out, she hugged her friend tightly and bit her bottom lip when Elizabeth briefly squeezed her back.

"You must be excited," the other woman said, forcing happiness into her tone.

"I am," Julia replied, wishing there was something she could say, something she could do, to make this less painful for Elizabeth. "And a little overwhelmed. It's all happening so quickly."

The pretty redhead gave her another wistful smile, then seemed to gather her inner strength while squaring her shoulders. "Enjoy it, Julia. Seriously. Make sure you take the time to enjoy every minute."

There it was again, that pang of sympathy, and everything in Julia yearned to ease the pain flickering in her friend's eyes. Some things, though, simply couldn't be helped by a warm hug or a heartfelt wish. "Elizabeth…would you like to come up for tea?"

"No. No, thanks." Elizabeth lifted her chin and forced a bright, yet brittle smile. "I've got to run. I'm meeting a friend for an early dinner and I don't want to keep her waiting."

"Sure," Julia said, realizing that Elizabeth was trying to make a hasty getaway. And who could blame her? "But if you ever need someone to talk to…"

"Thanks. I appreciate it, really. But I'm fine. We're fine. Reed and I, I mean." She took a breath, blew it out and said, "Now I'm babbling, so I'm gonna go." She took a few steps away, then stopped, looked back and said, "Just remember what I said and make sure you relish every minute of this, okay?"

Then, as if she'd said too much, Elizabeth hurried across the lobby and nearly beat Henry to the door in her haste to get outside.

Julia stepped into the elevator and noticed the faint scent of Elizabeth's perfume still hanging in the air. As the doors swept shut, Julia closed her eyes briefly and wondered where the justice in life was. Elizabeth wanted a child so badly, and the absence of a pregnancy was slowly destroying her happiness. And Julia was marrying a man who didn't love her because of a surprise pregnancy.

As the elevator lifted, she dropped one hand to her stomach and whispered, "Don't take it personally, though, little one. I *like* surprises."

Smiling to herself, Julia leaned back against the elevator wall and idly listened to the hum of the motor as she glanced through the mail she still held in one hand. She thumbed through the envelopes until she came to one that looked chillingly familiar.

Tearing open the flap on the plain white envelope with only her name scrawled across the front, Julia ripped the single sheet of paper from it and quickly scanned the words written there.

Congratulations on your so sudden marriage. You've escaped me. This time.

Seven

They left the lawyer's office and Max steered Julia out onto a crowded sidewalk. Pedestrians hustled past them, a few of them clearly irritated at being forced to walk around the couple, who only stood there and stared at each other.

"I want my own lawyers to look over the papers before I sign," Julia said for the third time since leaving Alex's office. "It's only reasonable."

"We don't have a lot of time," Max told her, taking her hand and dragging her out of the flow of foot traffic. He shifted until her back was against the dappled marble of the office building and his own body shielded hers from passersby. Then he looked down into the big blue eyes that had been haunting him for weeks.

He tried to read her thoughts, but for whatever reason, today she seemed able to disguise what she was thinking. Which only troubled him more than usual.

"You looked at the papers yourself. They're perfectly straightforward. What's the problem?"

"You're rushing me," she said, glancing to either side of her as if to assure herself that no one was paying them the slightest amount of attention. "I don't like to be rushed."

He laughed shortly. "You're the one with the tight schedule here." He shot a quick look at her flat belly and then lifted his gaze to meet hers again. "We want this marriage sewn up tight before you start showing, remember?"

She glowered at him and her eyes danced with sparks of anger. "I'm not going to sprout overnight, Max. Another day or two can't possibly make that much difference."

It did, though. To him. Since setting out on this path, Max had become more determined with every passing day to have her be his. Legally. He wasn't willing to look at why; all he knew was that he wanted her. In his bed. In his home. In his life. And he wasn't willing to give her a chance to change her mind and waltz out of his world as breezily as she'd waltzed into it.

"Who's your lawyer?" he asked. When she gave him the name of one of the city's top firms, Max nodded. "We'll go there right now."

"Max, I can take care of this myself."

"No reason you should have to," he said. "Besides,

you'll want to be at your apartment when the movers show up."

"That's another thing!" she snapped, lifting her chin and narrowing her eyes. "I didn't ask you to arrange for movers."

"You didn't have to. I saw what needed doing, so I did it. End of story."

"To you, maybe."

Max moved in closer as the crowds thickened behind him. Julia shot a nervous glance around her as if trying to find an escape route. As if he would allow that to happen. He bent his head to hers, and her eyes looked huge in her face. Her breath quickened and the pulse point at the base of her throat began to throb in time with her heartbeat.

Max smiled, enjoying the effect he had on her even while having to deal with how his own body responded to her nearness. Walking wasn't going to be comfortable for a while, but damned if he could force himself to back up any. The scent of her reached him and clawed at his self-control.

Lifting both hands to his chest, Julia gave him a shove that didn't move him an inch, then, disgusted, huffed out a breath. "Honestly, Max, you can't just take over my life."

One corner of his mouth lifted as he skimmed his fingertips along the side of her jaw. "You think that's what I'm trying to do?"

She batted his hand away. "Aren't you?"

"No," he said, and meant it. Hell, he liked her just

the way she was. Opinionated, stubborn, with a barely contained wild streak—which was the very reason she'd allowed herself to fall into bed with him the night they'd met.

He'd known from the moment he saw her that he wanted her. And the sparks between them had flown fast and furious that night. Still, he'd been surprised that Julia Prentice, society princess, had stepped out of her entrenched-in-rules life long enough to lose herself to passion.

That night had been a revelation to him. He'd seen beyond the facade she showed society to the woman she was beneath her well-tailored clothes and appropriate behaviors. And that was the woman who continued to haunt him. She was an intriguing blend of buttoned-down conventionality and uninhibited siren—and just standing this close to her made him hard and eager to have her again.

He wouldn't risk losing her now. Even if the marriage they were about to enter was a temporary one, he intended to get everything he could out of their time together. He wanted her. He wanted her child. He wanted it all.

And Max Rolland always got what he wanted.

"If you're not trying to steamroll me, then back off a little, Max."

He slapped one hand to the marble wall at her side. The cool stone was just beginning to warm up due to the wash of morning sunlight. From down the street came the mingled scents of car exhaust, coffee and hot dogs cooking on a cart. It was morning in New York City and the sights, scents and sounds surrounding him were like old friends.

Max smiled, stared into her eyes and said, "I'll back off as soon as we're married."

She frowned at him. "How do I know that?"

He shrugged. "Because I'm telling you I will."

"Oh," she said with a roll of her eyes, "well, that changes everything."

He smiled, enjoying the sarcasm, even enjoying the sparks still shooting from her eyes as she looked at him. Whatever else their businesslike marriage would be, it wouldn't be boring.

"Let's get this settled, all right? Get married. Get rid of the blackmailer and—" He stopped as her eyes widened and she inhaled sharply. "What is it?"

"The blackmailer," she said, opening up the long, narrow black leather bag she carried tucked beneath her arm. "I meant to tell you as soon as you arrived this morning, but you were so full of directives and commands, I forgot all about it."

He ignored that and demanded, "About what?"

She pulled an envelope from her purse and handed it to him. "This was in my mailbox yesterday."

Max pushed away from the wall, glared at the envelope and cursed viciously once he'd read the brief note. "So at the very least, this proves that whoever's behind this is privy to what goes on at 721."

"Apparently," she said, and this time when she looked at him, her eyes weren't shooting angry daggers at him, but were, instead, soft, confused and just a little worried. "How else would this person have known that I was getting married? And that they wouldn't be able to blackmail me now that I won't be pregnant and single?"

Scowling, Max took care to refold the letter and slide it back into its envelope. Then he tucked the missive into the inside pocket of his suit jacket and said, "You're right. Somehow this person is getting information about you. We haven't announced the wedding, so the only way they could have known is if they were somehow connected to 721. Either this person lives here, or knows someone who does."

"It could be anyone," she murmured.

"It could," he agreed, and sent a seeking glance out over the passing pedestrians as if he half expected to see a familiar face watching them. When he saw nothing, he drew Julia away from the building, dropped one arm around her shoulders and pulled her into his side. Then steering her into the moving, jostling throng, he bent his head to say, "Once we're married, the threat to you is over. I'll get this latest letter to Detective McGray, and you…"

"Yes?" She tipped her face up to look at him.

He gave her a half smile and said, "You can get the papers to your lawyer with orders to look them over quickly, then you can direct the movers. The quicker we get you settled at my place, the sooner you can put this behind you."

She frowned again, but nodded in agreement. "Fine.

I really hate to admit that you're right. But you are. At least about this."

Max raised one dark eyebrow as he looked down at her. "I think I just won the war."

"Not the war," she said, giving him a grudging smile that tugged at something inside him, "just this battle."

"For right now," he said, relishing the sweet tang of victory, "I'll settle for that."

"I can't believe all of your stuff is gone," Amanda said, turning in a slow circle in the middle of the living room. "It looks so…empty in here."

"I know." Julia sighed and dropped into one of the two remaining chairs. The movers Max had hired had, of course, been extremely diligent. They'd swept into the apartment, packed up everything she'd pointed at, then left to deliver it all to Max's penthouse. Julia had supervised, but her presence hadn't really been necessary. Within a few short hours, it was all handled and she was officially no longer a resident of 721 Park Avenue.

Which left her feeling a little odd. She'd loved her apartment. She had a lot of good memories wrapped up in this place. Now she was moving on, marrying the father of her child, preparing to be a mother and walking away from everything familiar and into a brand-new world.

Plus, she was leaving Amanda here in the very building where a blackmailer was running rampant. She was a little worried about her friend, though when she said so, Amanda pooh-poohed her.

"Oh, please," she said, pulling on a pair of short black boots. "What do I have going on in my poor, pitiful, loveless life that could interest a self-respecting blackmailer?"

"Fine, maybe you're right," Julia said, scooting forward until she was perched on the edge of the chair, arms braced on her knees, staring into her friend's guileless eyes. "But what if *Max* is right? What if this blackmailer had something to do with Marie Endicott's death?"

Amanda stilled for a minute, then reached up and ruffled her short blond hair with both hands until it looked stylishly tousled. "Okay, you had me there for a minute, but there's no proof that that poor woman was murdered. It's just as likely she either fell or jumped."

"I know but—"

"You may have a point," Amanda announced as she stood up, then pulled Julia to her feet, too. "But I'm not going to worry about something I can't change. I'll be careful, I swear, so don't worry. But I'm not going to spoil the pleasure of having this great apartment all to myself by scaring myself silly over what's probably nothing."

Julia smiled reluctantly. If Amanda wasn't too worried, then there was no reason for Julia to try to make her so. She settled for teasing her friend. "Fine. I can see that you're going to miss me horribly. You're already rubbing your hands together gleefully at the thought of living alone!"

"Oh, honey!" Amanda grinned, swept in and gave

Julia a quick, fierce hug. "That's not what I meant at all! Of course I'll miss you. Who will I have to join me in a midnight splurge on hot-fudge sundaes? Who will be here to listen to me moan and complain about my irritating clients? Who can I steal…er, borrow purses from?"

Julia shook her head and laughed. "Okay, I'm convinced I'm loved."

"You are, you know," Amanda said, her smile fading into seriousness. "And not just for your great purses and shoes, either, though they are a consideration. I'm really going to miss you now that you're moving in with Mad Max."

Julia laughed even harder. "Mad Max?"

Amanda shrugged. "It's how I think of him. I mean, come on. He's rough and rugged—so not one of the usual society types all cool and icy—and he's a little arrogant, which is just so sexy, don't you think?"

Julia did think so. The man oozed sex. All he had to do was walk into a room and she was ready to find the nearest flat surface. Although, even as that thought rolled through her mind, she remembered that only that morning, when he'd braced her against the office building, a part of her had wanted him to lean in and take her right there. Crowds or not. Busy city street or not. She didn't need a flat surface at all. She only needed him.

Not that she'd admit this to anyone else, of course.

"Humph," she said, with a wicked look at Amanda. "A week ago, you were warning me not to marry him."

"Well, as a best friend, that's my job. But since you *are* going to marry him and he *is* the father of your baby, let's at least admit that the man is a treat for the eyes."

"He is that," Julia said on a sigh. "And for other things, as well."

Amanda groaned and slapped one hand to her heart. "You're killing me here. Remember me? The not-by-choice celibate roommate?"

"Vaguely," Julia said, grinning, since she heard the self-deprecating tone in Amanda's voice quite plainly. After all, Amanda herself had chosen to steer clear of relationships after her last one had ended so badly.

"Fine, fine, make light of my pain." Amanda grabbed her purse, tossed Julia's black bag to her and said, "And now, to make up for showing so little sympathy for my lack of a sex life, you get to go shopping with me."

Julia tried to pull away and looked longingly at the chair she'd just left. "Amanda, I'm exhausted…"

"Nothing that a latte and a doughnut won't cure. My treat."

"Seriously, I've got to get to Max's. The movers have unloaded everything, but I've got to finish organizing my stuff and—"

"You can do that anytime," Amanda protested, already dragging Julia toward the door. "How many times will you get to help me buy a new couch? Oh, and tables. And maybe a couple of lamps. And what do you think about new drapes?"

Groaning, Julia followed in her friend's wake,

knowing there was no escape until Amanda's shopping bug had been fed.

As they stepped out of the elevator into the lobby, Amanda was promising her that latte before they got busy shopping. Both women stopped and smiled at Carrie Gray, waiting for the elevator.

At twenty-six, Carrie had gorgeous chestnut hair she forever tied back in a ponytail, big green eyes hidden behind a pair of glasses and a figure most women would kill for, nearly always disguised beneath oversize shirts and baggy jeans. A friendly woman, Carrie lived in apartment 12B but was officially a house sitter for Prince Sebastian Stone of Caspia. Carrie spent most of her time in the apartment, working on her sketches and trying to find a job doing what she loved.

Today, though, she looked exhausted. Even as Julia noticed the shadows under her friend's eyes, Carrie yawned and laughed at the same time.

"Sorry, sorry," she said, then blinked her eyes rapidly as if trying to wake herself up.

"Late night?" Amanda teased.

"Not the way you mean, unfortunately," Carrie admitted.

Behind them, the elevator closed with a quiet swish of sound and in the center of the lobby, Henry stood at his station, sparing the three of them only the barest glance.

Amanda was grinning. "You still having trouble with Trent's Troops?"

Julia groaned. The three of them had come up with

the title "Trent's Troops" for the mind-boggling string of women who came and went from Trent Tanford's apartment on a daily basis.

And, by the way Carrie's green eyes lit with fury, Julia guessed Amanda had been on target. Trent Tanford, heir to a huge entertainment empire, was a classic playboy. The man was far too handsome for his own good and regularly had women dropping at his feet. Unfortunately for Carrie, Trent's women wandered in and out of the building all night long, and apparently, most of them were confused enough to ring Carrie's bell in apartment 12B, instead of Trent's in 12C.

"Honestly, you guys," Carrie said, then checked her voice and lowered it so that Henry wouldn't overhear. Leaning forward, she said, "It's completely out of hand. That guy's got hot- and cold-running women all night long. What is he, a rabbit?"

Amanda laughed and even Julia had to smile, despite the fact that Carrie looked fit to kick something.

"Last night?" Carrie shook her head and her long ponytail whipped from side to side behind her. "The doorbell rings at 3:00 a.m. and there's this barely legal blonde standing there smiling at me like I'm the maid ready to usher her into the sex god's presence. Mind you, two other women have already gotten me up during the night. Apparently Trent can't find women who can read, since none of them can tell the difference between a *B* and a *C*. So I'm running on no sleep and zero patience by this time."

"Uh-oh," Julia muttered.

"Exactly," Carrie said, then continued with her story. "The blonde says, 'Hello, I'm Lauren Hunter,' as if I care who she is." Fisting her hands at her sides, Carrie took a deep breath as if just remembering the night before was churning her temper again. "So I'd had it. I just lost it with this woman. I yelled at her, told her she was at the wrong apartment and that if she was going to go get a quickie with Trent, then the least she could do was make sure she got his address right. For God's sake, is it really so hard to check before ringing somebody's doorbell in the middle of the night?"

"Good for you," Amanda said.

"Felt good, but she looked shocked," Carrie said. "The next time one of his bimbos knocks on my door looking for him, though, I'm not going to take it out on her. I swear I'm going straight to Trent and let *him* have it."

"Maybe you should," Julia said. "Maybe he doesn't know his women are disturbing you."

Carrie slid her a long look. "You really think Trent Tanford is worried about disturbing me? I don't think so. The man is interested in one thing only…"

She left the rest unsaid and, really, why not? They all knew the only thing Trent wanted from women.

Amanda reached out and gave Carrie a brief hug. "You want to come to Park Café with us and get a latte? I'll buy you a doughnut!"

Carrie chuckled, half turned and punched the up button on the elevator. "Thanks, but all I want right now is several uninterrupted hours of sleep."

As she and Amanda left the lobby of 721, Julia thought wistfully that now that she'd be living with Max full-time, she wouldn't have any more of these spur-of-the-moment conversations with her friends again. No more meeting in the elevator. No more chitchatting in the lobby. No more laughing with Amanda over late-night cookie binges.

Of course, there were compensations to living with Max that she didn't have now, too.

Say, for example, living with the man she loved. Although she knew he didn't love her back.

Eight

Julia pushed at the heavy, mahogany dresser and managed to move it a couple of inches along the gleaming wood floor. Then she stopped, huffed out an impatient breath and glared at the blasted thing as if it were being deliberately stubborn. You'd think the thing would slide a little more easily. It wasn't as if she was trying to push it into the next room, after all.

She stopped and looked around the master bedroom. Hers and Max's bedroom now. She wondered how it would be to fall asleep beside him every night and wake up next to him every morning. She smiled to herself as she silently acknowledged that in a bed that wide, they might not even notice each other's presence.

But as soon as that thought sped through her mind,

she discounted it. She was always hyper aware of Max, no matter where they were. Lying beside him in that big bed, she knew, was going to be both glorious and miserable. Julia never would have agreed to marry him, even for the rescue he offered her, if she didn't care for him. If she didn't love him.

How she'd managed to fall in love with Max Rolland so quickly, so irrevocably, was beyond her, but that step had been taken and there was no going back. Julia sighed a little as she stared at the bed covered in a dark red silk duvet, and she wondered if living with Max without his love was going to be a little like dying just a bit every day.

Her only recourse was not to let him see what she felt for him. To behave no differently than she ever had around him. And to hope that sometime during the year of their temporary marriage, he might come to love her, too.

"What're you doing?"

She jumped, startled, and spun around, one hand at her throat as she stared at her soon-to-be husband standing in the doorway. Her heart jolted a little and her insides began their now familiar twist into expectant knots. But with her latest resolution to keep what she felt for him to herself in mind, she blurted, "You scared me!"

"Same to you," Max snarled, glaring at her. He stalked into the master bedroom, marched directly up to her and grabbed hold of her right arm. He paid no attention at all to the electricity that zipped through his veins at the merest touch of her skin to his. He wasn't about to be sidetracked by desire. "I said, what're you doing?"

She pulled her arm free, gave him the same disgusted look she'd just directed at the dresser and quipped, "What am I doing? Brain surgery. You?"

"Funny," he said, not smiling in the least.

He'd arrived at the penthouse loft only a minute or so ago and had noticed the difference in his home the moment he walked in. There were bright, colorful throw pillows on the sofas and chairs in the living room. There were fashion magazines spread across the coffee table and a pair of high heels apparently kicked off in front of one of the couches.

But he hadn't even needed to see those physical hints of Julia's presence. Standing in the foyer, he'd *felt* the difference in the atmosphere instantly. Until today, every night when he walked into his empty home, he told himself it was as he wanted it. Privacy. Space. Time to think with no one making demands on him.

But with the simple act of moving into the penthouse, Julia had changed that. There was life here now. Even the air was faintly scented with her perfume. The rooms seemed warmer, the apartment itself more welcoming somehow. And he found he relished it. So naturally, he'd gone in search of his almost wife only to locate her in the bedroom, pushing a huge piece of furniture.

"Are you nuts?" he demanded, waving one hand at the dresser. "That thing's got to weigh a couple hundred pounds. What're you doing trying to move it by yourself?"

Both of her eyebrows lifted, she gave him a tight smile and, ignoring his bluster, turned to shove at the thing again as if he hadn't said a word. Max could hardly believe it. He wasn't accustomed to people disregarding what he said. And he didn't much care for it.

Max pulled her away, turned her around and held on to her shoulders with a viselike grip. "You're pregnant, Julia. You shouldn't be trying to move heavy furniture."

She sighed. "I'm not an invalid and the baby is perfectly safe."

"You're not doing this," he said and to avoid further argument, bent down, scooped her up into his arms and carted her over to the wide bed, where he dropped her on the mattress. She bounced a little and then looked up at him through narrowed blue eyes.

"Max, I'm perfectly capable of—"

"Where were you trying to move it to?" He cut her off as he walked quickly to the dresser.

She sighed again, shook her head and pointed. "There. Just a foot or two to your left."

Muttering darkly about women being unable to leave things as they were, he put his back to it and in moments had the dresser exactly where she wanted it. "There. Happy?"

"Deliriously."

He brushed back the edges of his jacket and planted both hands on his hips. "Why didn't you have the movers do that for you when they were here this morning?"

"Because I didn't think of it then." She scooted toward the edge of the bed, dragging the sumptuous duvet with her.

When she was on her feet again, Max walked toward her, looked down into her eyes and said, "I don't want you doing any heavy lifting or pushing. Understood?"

She tipped her head to one side and he tried not to notice how her blond hair looked lying against her throat. "Are you really worried, Max?"

Frowning, he studied her a long moment before saying, "Of course I am. You're going to be my wife. You're carrying the child who will be my heir."

"Wow," she said softly, wistfully. "That's just so special and touching."

His scowl deepened. Was that disappointment in her voice? What had she expected him to say? More importantly, what had she wanted him to say?

Then she was speaking again and Max reined in his thoughts. He'd already learned that it made good sense to pay attention when she was talking.

"I won't be coddled, Max," she said quietly. "I'm a big girl and I can take care of myself."

"You're pregnant."

"Yes," she said, smiling, "I know."

"I won't have you risking yourself or the baby with ridiculous stunts."

"Ridiculous?"

"That's right," he snapped, wondering where this

overprotective streak was coming from. All he knew was that when he'd seen her shoving a piece of furniture that weighed more than twice what she did, he'd felt something inside him break.

"If we're getting married, Max—"

"*If?*"

She ignored that and continued, "If we're getting married, then you might as well get used to the idea that I don't like being ordered around."

"That's a shame." Why was he still practically vibrating with a jumble of emotions he didn't really want to acknowledge? And why the hell was he issuing a deliberate challenge to a woman he knew damn well would fight him tooth and nail over it?

"Yes, it is. For *you.*" She took a step closer to him, shook her hair back from her face and lifted her chin so that her gaze could spear his more easily.

He knew she was trying to look steely, immovable. But damned if he didn't find those glints in her eyes so sexy he wanted to tumble her backward onto the bed.

"I'm perfectly capable of taking care of myself."

"You're marrying me," he told her, his voice low and hard. "That makes taking care of you *my* responsibility."

She actually smiled briefly, but the expression didn't have a trace of amusement in it. "You sound like a medieval prince or something."

"I can live with medieval," he said, nodding at the image.

"Well, I can't."

"Is it so hard for you to accept help?"

She blew out a breath that ruffled a strand of hair falling across her eyes. "I don't mind *help,* Max," she said, keeping her gaze locked on his as if trying to will him to understand what she meant. "I came to you in the first place because I needed help, and somehow, I knew instinctively that you would be there for me."

Something in Max's chest tightened at those soft words, so simply spoken. In business, Max knew his allies and even his competitors respected him. Knew that once given, his word could be trusted. But in his personal life, he'd been stung badly and so had pulled back from making the kinds of commitments women wanted.

He'd considered himself cold, withdrawn and had thought himself at peace with himself. Yet, those few words from Julia meant more to him than he wanted to admit. The wall of ice around his heart seemed to splinter, jagged shards of the damn thing slicing at his insides. But as the pain tugged at him, a corner of Max's mind, still logical, still fighting the sexual pull dragging at him, whispered, *She came to you because she knew you'd help her even though she's pregnant with another man's baby. She came to you for help, but lied to you to get it. Why? Because she knew you'd come through for her, or because she thought a society princess was doing the common man a favor?*

But did it matter?

He'd gotten what he wanted.

Her. And the heir he'd craved. A part of him still

wondered about the father of her baby. If he'd come back. Change his mind and demand rights to the child Max was already thinking of as his own. And if this nameless sperm donor changed his mind about his baby, wouldn't he also want Julia? Who the hell *wouldn't* want Julia?

His brain raced as he walked to her, every step measured. His gaze locked on her as he told himself he'd never give her up. Never let her go back to the man who'd left her pregnant and alone. She was his now. As was the child.

The closer he came to her, the more he felt that territorial surge pumping through him. *His.* One word, it echoed over and over again in his mind. Julia Prentice would be his wife. Her baby would be his heir. And he'd ruin *anyone* who tried to change that.

His body was hard, his blood was thick and hot in his veins, and the racing thoughts in his mind scattered like autumn leaves in a high wind. She was too close for him to be thinking about anything but having her. Drowning in her eyes, losing himself in her body, surrendering to the incredible rush of heat and longing that sprang into being whenever he saw her.

"I will be there for you and the baby," he finally said, fighting the urge to grab her, hold her, take her mouth with all the hunger pumping inside him. "And since I'm now that baby's father, I'm not going to stand back and watch you endanger the baby without saying something."

"I wouldn't endanger my child," she argued, her gaze caught in his, her body leaning toward him.

"I know," he allowed. Silently he asked himself where this was coming from. Why just looking at her made him alternately want to wrap her up and make sure she was safe and at the same time strip her down and lose himself in the glory that was her body. But any answer he might come up with would only jangle his nerves more than the question, so he let it go.

"Are you going to be giving me orders for the next seven months?" Her eyes glittered, reflecting the soft lamplight in the room, and Max felt as though he couldn't breathe when he looked at the deep blue of those eyes shining at him.

He blew out a breath. "Probably," he admitted, then added, "Look, I know you wouldn't do anything deliberately to hurt yourself or the baby. But you can't do everything you used to do without stopping to think of the possible consequences."

A minute of silence hummed between them, fraught with emotions neither of them were willing to admit to. Seconds ticked past and Max had to fight the urge to pull her close to him. To bend his head, taste her lips, strip her down and lose himself in the feel of her beneath his hands.

Finally she said, "You're right."

"Now, there's something I never thought I'd hear you say again." One corner of Max's mouth turned up. "I think we're having a moment here."

She laughed a little, shook her head and warned, "Don't get used to it."

Max lifted one hand, cupped her cheek and stared

directly into her eyes. Then he spoke, a soft warning for both of them. "Maybe neither one of us should get too used to this."

"This?"

"Being together."

"We will be, though," she reminded him. "For a year, anyway."

He smiled again and stroked the tips of his fingers over her cheekbone. A year of Julia in his life. In his home. In his bed. Did it matter that she'd lied to him to bring them to this point? No, it didn't. Not to him. She'd lied, but she'd done it for her child. That he could understand. Hell, admire. And it had brought her here. To him.

"So you've decided to sign the papers, then?"

"Yes." Her gaze shifted to one side briefly before coming back to meet his again. He felt that powerful blue gaze punch into him, and the hunger inside roared with a need that nearly brought him to his knees.

"My lawyer went over them this afternoon," she said. "I signed them. Left them on the dining-room table."

A knot of tension he hadn't been aware he was carrying dissolved inside him, and Max threaded his fingers through her hair at her temple. The silken strands slid against his skin, warming him, tempting him—as if he needed further tempting.

"Good," he said, and heard the husky note of need in his own voice. "That's good. So it's official. We're a couple."

"A trio, actually," she said, her smile fading into an expression of desire as his fingers continued to slide through her hair.

"I stand corrected," he whispered, lowering his head to hers. "I also stand hungry."

"Dinner's in the fridge," she murmured, twisting her head into his hand, so that she could feel more of him. "Your housekeeper left it and—"

"That's not what I'm hungry for," Max said, and took her mouth with his. It began as a gentle brush of his lips on hers, then quickly became something much more. Something he found he desperately needed.

She leaned into him and Max caught her up, pulling her close, molding her body to his, feeling the need inside him clawing for release. He groaned as the taste of her filled him, swamping him, drowning him in sensation that only grew more complex, more overpowering. Her scent wafted around him, teasing his every breath with another layer of *her.*

His hands swept up and down her spine, feeling every curve, defining every line. The taste of her swam through him in a rush of something so powerful his mind quieted, his thoughts faded, and he gave himself up to the moment.

She sighed and his heartbeat quickened. She leaned into him, wrapped her arms around his neck, and everything in him roared. He broke their kiss, tearing his mouth from hers, only to move to her jaw and trail hot, damp kisses down the length of her slender throat. When he reached that pulse-pounding point at the base of her neck, he tasted the evidence of *her* need. The frantic beating of her heart, the staggering sighs of her breathing.

Julia groaned, allowing that one small sound to slide from her throat into the stillness of the room. The touch of his hands was like fire. Her head dropped back and she stared blankly at the ceiling as Max's mouth moved up and down her throat, trailing hot, urgent kisses. His hands swept over her, sliding beneath the hem of her shirt, tugging it up and over her head. Once he had the silky garment in his hands, he tossed it over his shoulder to land on the floor. Then he flipped the catch on her bra, slid it off and down her shoulders and filled his hands with her breasts. His thumbs smoothed across her hardened nipples until Julia was nearly whimpering with the sensations coursing through her.

He walked her backward until the backs of her thighs hit the edge of the massive bed. His gaze locked with hers, she couldn't look away. Couldn't seem to see anything but the green eyes watching her, devouring her.

Ribbons of need unwound inside her, and Julia surrendered to the inevitable. When he laid her back on the bed, she felt the cool slide of silk against her bare skin. She lifted her hips as Max unhooked her slacks, slid the zipper down and then pulled them down her legs. All she wore now was a scrap of pale pink lace underwear that was gone in the next second. Naked, hungry for the sight of him, the feel of him, she scooted farther back on the bed and watched as he quickly stripped off his own clothes, his gaze never leaving hers.

"I want you," he whispered as he joined her on the bed, sliding his big hands up her calves, her thighs, her hips. "I always want you. It's like fire in the blood. Never quenched, never satisfied, always burning."

"I know," she said, reaching for him, tugging his mouth down to hers. "I know just what that feeling is like. It's never been like this for me before. Only with you."

"Only me," he repeated, and dipped his head for a quick kiss. But when she tried to hold him there, hungry for the taste of him, he escaped her grasping hands and moved, trailing hot, damp kisses along her body. He gave each of her tender, sensitive nipples attention, then moved on, sliding lower and lower over her body until Julia was twisting and writhing beneath him, eager for what she knew was coming, what she wanted desperately.

He knelt between her thighs, scooped his hands beneath her bottom and lifted her until her legs dangled free and she was helpless in his grasp. "Max…" She swallowed hard, took a breath and held it.

"I want the taste of you in my mouth. I want all of you," he whispered. Then he bent his head to the core of her and flicked his tongue over that one small, too-sensitive spot.

Sparks shot through her bloodstream and exploded behind her eyes in a dazzling shower of light and heat. Again and again, he used his tongue to lick and stroke and gently torture her. She rocked her hips, grabbed fistfuls of the silken duvet beneath her and held on with an iron grip. The world seemed to teeter around her, spinning wildly out of control, and it was all due to the man so intimately loving her.

He pushed her higher, higher, and Julia fought for air. Fought to reach that peak he kept her climbing for. Tension coiled, tightening until she couldn't think, couldn't breathe, could only feel. When release came, her climax slammed into her, and Julia rocked helplessly in his grasp, riding the wave of completion that seemed to roll on forever.

"Max—"

"Not finished yet," he promised, and laid her down on the bed. Her body was still humming, still trembling with the force of her orgasm when Max turned her over and she lay facedown on the cover. She turned her head to one side and watched him as he stroked his hands up and down her spine until finally bringing them to rest at her hips.

He lifted her until she was on her knees and Julia felt a brand-new surge of want filling her. Amazing. She hadn't even stopped trembling from her last climax, and already, her body hungered for another. For the feel of his body pushing into hers, for the sensation of being filled by him.

"Take me, Max," she whispered, arching her back, offering herself to him. "I want you inside me."

He braced his thighs on either side of her and she felt the hard, warm strength of him surrounding her, claiming her. Then he leaned his body over hers and pushed himself into her depths.

Julia called out his name and pushed backward, meeting his thrusts, taking him deeper and more fully into her body than she ever had before. Again and again, he withdrew and entered, claiming more of her heart and soul with every slow thrust.

He moved one hand around her body and cupped her breast as he took her higher and higher. She moved with him, loving the feel of his hard, strong body covering hers, filling hers. She gave herself up to the wonder of it, and when her body exploded into glittering shards of pleasure, her breath shattered and she didn't breathe again until she felt him join her on that blissful slide into nothingness.

Nine

They settled into a routine of sorts over the next few days. With the wedding getting closer with every passing day, there were details to be dealt with and Max was astonished by how easily Julia managed everything.

On Monday she had a fitting for her wedding dress.

On Tuesday she dragged Max to the caterer Amanda had recommended.

On Wednesday they visited three florists with Amanda until a decision had been made.

On Thursday the judge who would perform the ceremony met with them to discuss what would be a brief, civil service.

And on Friday they had to attend a charity ball for the Midtown Shelter, one of the organizations Julia raised funds for.

Max hated wearing a tuxedo.

Somehow, they always made him feel like a fraud. Glancing around the room at the glittering stars of society, gathered together to be admired for the money they were donating, he felt like just what he was. A blue-collar kid from upstate New York.

It didn't seem to matter that he had more money than most of the attendees. Didn't matter that he'd worked for more than a decade, building his company into one of the fastest-growing financial institutions in the country. Didn't even matter that he was soon to be marrying into one of the oldest families in New York.

Because at gatherings like these, there were always the sidelong glances directed at him. The barely concealed snubs. These people might need his financial advice, but they didn't consider him one of them. And they never would.

Normally at one of these functions Max made the rounds, spoke to a few people, handled his donation and left, usually with some sparkling, empty-headed beauty on his arm. Tonight, though, everything was different.

His gaze focused on the reason.

Even from across the room, one glance at Julia and Max's body went hard and hot. She wore an off-the-shoulder, sapphire-blue gown with a low-cut bodice and a back that dipped so low, you could almost see the top of her behind. Her hair was done up on top of her head into a mass of curls, and her blue eyes shone with excitement and satisfaction.

She'd worked hard to pull this night off and Max felt a stir of admiration for her. His gaze followed her as she worked the crowd. A smile here, a brief touch on the shoulder there, a quick word and a laugh with an older man and she was moving again, sifting through the crowd, the rich hue of her gown soaking up the overhead lights and making her shine in a roomful of crows.

All around him, the hum of conversations rose and fell like the ocean's waves. The air smelled of expensive perfume and the banks of roses that studded the walls. At one end of the massive ballroom, an orchestra was tuning up and at the other end, an incredible buffet was laid out to tempt appetites. Caterers moved through the crowd offering trays laden with crystal glasses of champagne, yet Max hardly noticed any of it.

His gaze was solely for Julia. She was a part of this crowd as he never would be. She belonged to it. But, he thought with an inner smile as he took a sip of champagne, she also belonged to him.

"Don't look now," a deep voice said from right beside him, "but you're drooling."

Max laughed shortly, shot his friend a quick look, then turned his gaze back to Julia as she continued her parade through the milling throng. "Alex," he said. "Didn't know you'd be here."

"Oh," Alex Harper said, "I show up at these things occasionally."

"Surprised you were willing to take time from work." Max knew only too well that his friend's devotion to work rivaled his own.

"Believe me," Alex told him, "this is work." He accepted a glass of champagne from a passing waiter, took a sip and said, "Do you have any idea how boring it is listening to some of these people?"

"Yeah, I do." Max's eyes narrowed. Julia had stopped alongside a tall, blond guy who looked as if he'd just stepped off the cover of *GQ*.

"Still," his friend went on, "you've got to take the time to see clients in social settings once in a while."

"Uh-huh." Did she have to lay her hand on the guy's arm?

"Clients expect some personal treatment outside the office, too."

"Sure." She was smiling now, leaning into the blond guy so he could kiss her cheek. What the hell was that about?

"And then sometimes the clients want me to train their camels to do a high-wire act for the circus."

"Yeah, I know." Kissing *both* cheeks? Who was this guy?

Beside him Alex laughed and clapped a hand to Max's shoulder. "You've got it bad, don't you."

"Huh? What?" Tearing his gaze from Julia and her new "friend," Max glared at Alex. "What did you say about camels?"

"Nothing." Alex shook his head, reached out and took Max's champagne glass, then said, "The music is starting. Why don't you go get that gorgeous woman before you pop a blood vessel or something."

Scowling, Max shoved both hands into his pants pockets. "I don't know what you're talking about."

"Sure, you don't." Alex laughed a little. "For God's sake, Max, if looks could kill, that guy would be six feet under and stone-cold."

"Who the hell is he?"

"Who cares? She's not engaged to him. She's going to marry *you*. So go ask her to dance."

"Since when did you start giving advice on women?"

Alex laughed again. "I'm always ready to *give* advice. It's the taking of it where I draw the line."

When Alex walked away, Max shifted his gaze back to the woman currently driving him insane. The blond guy was still standing too close, and Julia still appeared to enjoy talking to him. So maybe Alex was right. Maybe it was time to remind both Julia and her friend just who she'd come here with tonight.

Making his way through the crowd, Max stopped alongside Julia and felt a flicker of pleasure when she grinned up at him and immediately linked her arm through his. "Max, hi. I was just telling Trevor about you."

Trevor.

"Is that right?" His voice came out a little harsher, stiffer, than he'd planned, and the quick flash of worry in Julia's eyes forced Max to lighten up as he held out one hand to Trevor. "Max Rolland."

The other man shook his hand and said, "Trevor Swift. I hear congratulations are in order." He beamed at Julia. "You're getting a hell of a woman."

Max drew Julia closer to his side. "I think so. How do you two know each other?"

"Oh, our families have been friends for years," Julia said quickly.

"Yes," Trevor admitted. "Julia and I used to go off together to avoid our parents whenever we could."

"Is that right?" Looking into the eyes of the man smiling at him, Max felt a sharp stab of something unexpected. Something unfamiliar. Jealousy. Trevor and Julia had grown up together, in the same social circle. A part of Max resented the fact that this guy knew the woman he would be marrying far better than he himself did.

"Having Julia around was the one thing that kept me sane when dealing with my parents," Trevor was saying, clearly unaware of Max's slow burn.

"I'm sure," he said, fighting the urge to plant a fist into the man's smiling face, just to let him know that Julia was taken now.

"Um, Max?" Julia tugged at his arm until she had his attention.

He shifted his gaze to hers and saw uneasiness flickering in her eyes. Was he so easy for her to read, then? Forcing a smile, he bent, kissed her quickly, then straightened and said, "You'll have to excuse us, Trevor. I want to dance with my fiancée."

"Of course, of course."

But Max wasn't listening. He'd already turned to steer Julia through the mass of people toward the dance floor. He swung her into his arms as the music swelled. It was an old tune from the forties, soft, dreamy.

She slid her left hand up his arm to lie on his shoulder and followed his lead smoothly as other couples joined them in a swirl of color and motion. His right hand lay at the small of her back, and the feel of her skin against his palm sent bolts of desire shooting through him.

Holding her right hand in his left, he gave her fingers a squeeze, looked down into her eyes and said, "So you and Trevor are close?"

"Yes," she said, her voice pitched just high enough to be heard over the swell of the orchestra but not loud enough to be overheard. "Since we were kids. His parents and mine have been friends for years, so Trev and I spent a lot of time together growing up."

"He loves you." The signs had been unmistakable. The warmth in the other man's eyes. The timbre of his voice when he spoke about her.

"I love him, too," she said, and sent a sharp knife through Max's chest. The pain was only alleviated a little when she added, "He's like my brother, Max."

He moved her into a tight turn that sent the skirt of her gown swirling about her legs. She moved closer to him, pressing her breasts to his chest, and Max could have sworn he felt her heart pounding against his.

"Are you jealous?"

He scowled down at her. "Apparently."

She smiled, damn it.

"If the two of you are so tight," he asked because he had to know, "why didn't you go to him when you needed a husband? Why come to me?"

A dizzying array of emotions darted across her features in a moment's time. Frustration, disappointment and anger merged together to set off a glint in her eyes that signaled her own temper beginning to build.

"A couple of reasons," she told him. "First, being that it's *your* baby I'm carrying…"

He rolled his eyes and shook his head. "And?"

"And," she repeated, bending her head closer to his, lowering her voice dramatically, "Trev's gay, Max. His parents don't know, but he lives with a lovely man named Arthur. Somehow I didn't think Arthur would be pleased to have me marry the man he considers to be *his* husband."

Relief swept through Max in such a rush it nearly stole his breath. Then in the next instant, he felt a tug of sympathy for the other man. If Max felt like an outsider at one of these things, how much more did a man like Trevor feel? Max at least could be himself and those who didn't like it were free to move on.

But Trevor couldn't even be himself with his family.

Staring down into Julia's eyes, Max frowned a little and said, "I thought—"

"I know what you thought," she said softly, shaking her head slightly and sending her mass of blond curls into a dance of their own. "Max, you have to trust me or we have nothing. This marriage won't even last out the year if you can't believe in me."

"Trust isn't something I give lightly."

"What have I done that makes you think you *can't* trust me?"

The music ended and he drew them to a stop. Looking down into her glimmering blue eyes, he said, "You won't tell me the truth about your baby."

"I have—"

"Don't keep trying to tell me it's mine," he whispered, the words scraping his throat as he spoke them. "I know different."

She let her hand fall from his shoulder and Max felt the absence of her touch as clearly as he'd felt the touch itself. "How can I make you believe me?"

"You can't."

"Then why are you going to marry me? If you won't trust me, can't believe in me, why do you want me?"

When the music rose again in another ballad designed to lure couples onto the dance floor, Max pulled her into his arms again. Holding her tightly to him, he allowed her to feel the hard eagerness in his body. When her eyes widened, he said gruffly, "Because you do that to me with a look. Because you walk into a room and everything but you disappears. Because you're *mine*."

The next hour or so flew by in a whirl. Julia felt Max's gaze on her wherever she went. As she talked to the caterers, schmoozed with patrons, dealt with any number of minor problems, Max's gaze filled her with heat.

And while she did everything that was expected of her, Julia's mind raced with the implications of her last conversation with Max. He didn't trust her. And that fact stung. All her life, Julia had been the kind of woman people could depend on. She prided herself on giving her word and keeping it. Now, knowing that the one man who *should* have believed her didn't, she felt more hurt than she wanted to admit.

"Good evening, Julia."

She stiffened, plastered a hard, tight smile on her face and turned to greet the woman behind that icy voice. "Hello, Mother. I didn't expect to see you here tonight."

Actually, that wasn't true. She'd been hoping not to see her parents. But the way her luck was running lately, their presence wasn't really a surprise.

"Of course we came," her mother said, sniffing delicately, then turning her head to observe the crowd. "Our friends would have missed us if we'd stayed away. And that would have led to questions we prefer not to answer."

So her parents hadn't resigned themselves yet to her upcoming wedding, Julia thought.

"I suppose your paramour is here," her mother said.

"If you mean my fiancé, then yes, Max is here tonight."

Margaret Prentice shuddered and the column of gold silk she wore wrapped about her too-thin frame rippled with the motion. "Your fiancé."

"Mother—"

"I won't discuss this with you, Julia. Not until you've come to your senses and called off this travesty of a marriage with a completely unsuitable man."

"Present," Max said suddenly from directly behind Julia.

She felt the heat of his body, the hard, solid strength of him behind her, and silently thanked him for coming to her aid.

"I beg your pardon?" Margaret asked, lifting her gaze to meet his.

"You were speaking about Julia's completely unsuitable fiancé. That would be me." He reached around Julia with his right hand while dropping his left hand onto her shoulder in an unmistakable claim. "Max Rolland, Mrs. Prentice."

Margaret briefly lowered her gaze to his outstretched hand, then pointedly ignored it. "I have nothing to say to you, Mr. Rolland. This is a private conversation between my daughter and myself."

Julia felt embarrassed. For her mother. For Max. For herself. This situation could only disintegrate and she wondered how to avoid what was bound to be more unpleasantness. All her life, she'd been alone against her parents' rigorous expectations and cold disapproval. She'd faced them both countless times and had always come away from the encounters feeling as though she would never measure up.

Now, she stiffened her shoulders, lifted her chin and prepared herself for what she knew was coming. Her mother's icy displeasure.

Then Max let his hand drop to wind about Julia's waist, pulling her back tightly against him. Margaret Prentice winced at the unseemly public display, but

Julia was grateful for the arm he kept wrapped around her. His broad, muscular chest was at her back and the solid thump of his heartbeat was a reminder that she wasn't alone. She didn't have to put up with her parents' dissatisfaction anymore. It was as if silently, Max was reminding her that times had changed. She wasn't a young girl desperately seeking support. She was a grown woman now, more than able to think and choose for herself. And the man she'd chosen stood behind her in a blatant display of solidarity she was more than grateful for.

"Anything you have to say to Julia, you can say in front of me."

"Julia, please tell this individual to leave."

"No."

Margaret's eyes widened and she couldn't have looked more stunned if Julia had reached out and slapped her.

"Excuse me?"

"I said no, Mother," Julia repeated, enjoying herself even more the second time. "I'm here with Max and we're busy right now."

Margaret's small, pinched mouth tightened even further, until her lips nearly disappeared from her face entirely. "This is unacceptable, Julia."

Around them, several heads began to turn their way, as if sensing gossip-worthy news.

Max must have noticed because just then, he smiled and said, "You're right, Mrs. Prentice. This is unacceptable. This is neither the time nor the place for this kind of conversation. So, if you'll excuse us, I think I'll just steal Julia away for another dance."

"My daughter and I are—"

"Finished talking," Max interrupted, leaving the older woman's mouth opening and closing like a landed trout gasping for air.

Before Julia could really enjoy the image, though, Max swept her away, pulled her into his arms and led her into a slow, romantic dance. Soon enough, Julia's mother was the furthest thing from her mind.

"Thank you," Julia said hours later as he entered their bedroom.

"For what?" He tore off his elegantly tied bow tie and tossed it negligently onto the nearest chair.

"For coming to my rescue," Julia said, stepping out of her high heels and nearly groaning with the pleasure of being barefoot. "With my mother."

Max shrugged out of his jacket, then unbuttoned his vest and shirt. "Not a problem. Felt good to leave her standing there staring after us."

When she didn't say anything, he looked at her. "Was she always like that?"

"Like what?"

"Cold."

"Yes." Julia couldn't remember a single moment in her life when either of her parents had offered her affection or even warmth. There had always been a careful distance between the Prentices and the child they hadn't really wanted.

Julia reached behind her for the zipper at the back of her dress, and when she couldn't quite get it, she walked to Max and turned so he could do it. She sucked in a breath as the backs of his fingers came into contact with her skin. With the zipper undone, the sapphire gown dropped to the floor between them and Max bent to pick it up for her.

"Can't imagine growing up like that," he muttered, sliding one hand across her behind, then around to the front, to dip his fingers beneath the slim band of elastic at the top of her black thong.

"It wasn't easy," she admitted, sighing a little as he stroked her skin.

"You did it, though," he whispered, bending to kiss the curve of her shoulder. "You survived them. And became an amazing woman."

Warmth settled in her chest and tears stung the backs of her eyes. "Thank you for that, too."

"I had family," he said, still moving his hand up and down the column of her spine. "Parents who loved me. Pushed me. Supported me."

"You were lucky."

"I know. Which is why I admire you even more than I did before. Everything you are," he said softly, his breath dusting across her neck and shoulder, "is your own doing. You owe them nothing."

His words filled her heart, his touch filled her soul, and Julia leaned back into him, suddenly needing him more than she ever had before.

"You're beautiful," he murmured.

"Max," she said, arching into his touch.

"I want you again."

"I know," she whispered, feeling the heat of his skin seep into her own. She hissed in a breath as his fingertips slid lower, lower, until he found that already heated bud of flesh at the heart of her.

"I wanted you at the party, too," he said softly, dipping his head to the curve of her neck. "I wanted to hold you like this."

"Max…" Julia's mind splintered as he began to move his fingers in and out of her heat. She parted her thighs for him and leaned back against him, counting on him to support her even as he tormented her.

"Don't talk for a minute, okay?" His words were muffled against her skin as he slowly moved, turning her in his arms until they were facing the mirror over the dresser.

Only one dim light burned in the room, and the glow of it wasn't bright enough to dispel the shadows crouched in the corners. Outside the expanse of windows, Manhattan lay covered in night, with the lights of the city sparkling like jewels. A nearly full moon shone in the distance, sending pearly silver light streaming into the bedroom, and in its glow, Julia looked at Max and her reflected in the mirror.

He was so much bigger than she. Broad in the shoulders, arms muscled and tanned against her white skin. He was dark where she was fair and the differences between them lay starkly revealed as he met her gaze in the mirror.

"Watch," he whispered, and with a quick twist of his wrist, tore her thong free and let it float to the floor. "Watch what I can do to you. What you do to me."

She couldn't look away. Couldn't tear her gaze from the couple in the mirror. He moved his left arm over her shoulder and cupped her breast in his palm. His right hand slid over her abdomen, caressing, stroking. His strong, tanned hands looked erotic sliding across her so-white skin, and Julia rubbed herself against him in response to the image they made.

"I want to touch you. And I want you to watch me pleasure you."

"Max…" She licked dry lips and watched with an avid gaze as his right hand slid lower and lower until he was once more stroking that tight bud of sensation between her thighs.

Again and again, his big hand dipped into her heat and she widened her stance, went up on her toes as he touched her. His left hand tweaked and tugged at her nipple while his right hand did amazing things to her core. She was hot all over. Her skin felt as if it were on fire. She rocked against him, teetering on her toes. Reaching back, she hooked one arm around his neck and closed her eyes.

"Open them," he demanded, and when she did, she met his heated gaze in the glass. She read hunger there and knew an answering hunger was in her own eyes. What he did to her was magic. What he made her want was more than she'd ever thought possible.

Tingles of expectation awoke inside her and she

knew she was poised on the very lip of a climax that would shatter her. While she watched, unable, unwilling, to look away now, he slid first one finger and then two inside her while his thumb continued to stroke and rub that one spot that ached for completion.

She watched herself writhe in his grasp and felt wild for the first time in her life. She wasn't controlled, wasn't thinking about anything but the effect Max had on her body. Every cell was alive and singing. Every nerve in her body jangled with bright anticipation. Her breath strained as she focused on the spiraling tension inside her, giving herself up to the frantic, driving need.

When the first shattering wave struck her, she screamed his name, looked into Max's reflected gaze and let him see everything he was doing to her. And when her body stilled, the last of the tremors fading into memory, he swept her into his arms and carried her to the wide, silk-covered mattress.

Much later, when she lay in his arms, both she and Max absolutely spent and cocooned in their bed, Julia traced his broad chest with the tips of her fingers, tangling them in the thatch of dark curls. Her body was sated, but her mind couldn't rest. Now that the fiery passion between them had been eased for the moment, there was something she had to know.

He'd stood alongside her tonight, allying himself with her against her mother. He'd given her his support, played the part of the loving fiancé in public and was the lover she'd always dreamed of in private. Still, he held back from her. Distanced himself. Refused to believe in the possibility that the child she carried was his. She had to find out his reasons for shutting her out.

"Max," she whispered, "I need you to tell me why you won't believe me about the baby."

He sighed, came up on one elbow and looked down at her. In the wash of moonlight, his green eyes shone like emeralds under a spotlight. His dark hair tumbled across his forehead and his mouth was tight and hard. "You're not going to let this go, are you?"

She shook her head on the pillow and met his gaze squarely. Reaching up, she cupped his cheek in her palm and brushed her thumb across his skin. "I can't, Max."

"Fine." Staring directly into her eyes, he said, "I've known from the beginning that you're lying to me. I can't be the baby's father, Julia. See, when she couldn't get pregnant, my ex-wife and I had all the tests done. I found out then that I'm infertile. I'm *nobody's* father."

Ten

"You're wrong." She looked confused. "There was a mistake. You have to go back to the doctor. Take the test again."

"What would be the point?" Max shook his head and blew out a frustrated breath. Finding out that he would never be able to father a child had cut at the very heart of him.

Even now, he remembered the sense of failure that had filled him when he was faced with the indisputable facts. That Julia could cling to her lies even when she knew the truth was astonishing. Looking into her eyes now, Max said, "Let it go, Julia. You don't need the lies. We're getting married. I'm going to adopt your child. At least let's have truth between us."

"I *am* telling you the truth."

Her eyes didn't flicker. She didn't look away. She didn't bite her lip or show any other sign that what he'd said had changed anything for her. So what the hell was she after? Why was she clinging to this ridiculous story?

Wasn't it enough that they were getting married? He was going to give her and her baby his name. Why couldn't she at least treat him with some respect? Give him the courtesy of some damn honesty?

"I've got some work I should be doing," he said, and pulled away from her, edging off the bed.

"Max, stay with me."

He glanced at her and saw she was sitting up, the silk duvet pooled in her lap, her breasts brushed by moonlight. Her pale hair was tumbled across her shoulders and she looked the image of every man's dream lover. There was nothing he wanted more than to get back into bed with her. To have her beneath him, his body locked with hers.

Because he wanted it so much, he ignored the urge and stalked naked across the room to the walk-in closet. There, he grabbed a thick, black cashmere robe and shrugged into it. When he stepped back into the bedroom, she hadn't moved. She was still sitting there, bathed in moonlight, watching him, a wordless plea in her eyes.

"Go to sleep," he said tightly, already headed for the door, since he didn't trust himself to stay too long. "I'll see you in the morning."

He closed the bedroom door behind him, and alone in the darkened hallway, he walked to his office, trying to put that last image of her out of his mind.

A part of Julia wanted to give up. To throw in the towel and just admit that Max would never be the husband she wanted him to be. How could they have *anything* together if he didn't believe her about something as big, as basic, as their child?

Her mind had been whirling for days. Ever since their late-night conversation when Max had told her what he believed to be the truth. She couldn't find a way past the wall he'd erected around himself and she was half-afraid she never would. And if she couldn't, what did that signify? Maybe she should rethink this marriage. Walk away and take her chances with the blackmailer.

Everything inside her cringed away from that idea. Yes, times had changed and single mothers were no longer the social pariahs they once had been. But Julia didn't want to do that to her baby. She wanted her child to have *two* parents. To be loved. To grow up surrounded by support and safety.

Besides, she thought, as she glanced around what was now Amanda's apartment, she couldn't move back in here. Her friend was so happy with the place and had already turned it into her own private nest.

"Did I tell you?" Amanda called from the kitchen, interrupting Julia's thoughts. "Elizabeth Wellington hired me to plan her and her husband's five-year anniversary party."

"That's great," Julia said, hoping she'd forced enough enthusiasm into her voice.

"I know! Although," Amanda added as she walked back into the living room, carrying two tall glasses of soda over ice, "between you and me, Elizabeth didn't look happy."

"What's wrong?"

"I don't think she meant to let this slip, so keep it between us, okay?"

"Of course."

Amanda handed her one of the glasses and said, "Elizabeth is worried that she shouldn't be celebrating a marriage she's afraid won't last another year."

"Oh, God. Poor Elizabeth. This has all been so hard on her." Julia took a sip of her soda and let the icy bubbles slide down her throat.

"She looked so sad for a minute, then she plastered on a smile and went back to talking about the party. Almost makes me feel guilty for taking the job."

"No," Julia said softly. "Just make it a great party. For her sake. I so know what Elizabeth is feeling. Sometimes we simply have to go through with something even when we've got doubts."

"That has the ring of personal experience."

Julia looked at her friend's concerned gaze and couldn't hide her feelings. Amanda knew her too well and wouldn't be fooled even if Julia tried. But the truth was, she needed to talk to someone about all this, and who better than her best friend?

"Max won't listen to me," Julia said, curling up on

one of the new chairs Amanda had purchased for the apartment. Her fingertips idly traced the outline of a pink cabbage rose on the arm of the overstuffed chair, but she wasn't really seeing it. Her mind was filled with the image of Max's face as he'd called her a liar. Again.

"This surprises you?" Amanda took a seat in the chair opposite her. "You knew going into this that he was stubborn. Heck, the man's made his name on Wall Street by being the hardest-headed man in the country. Everyone says that once he makes up his mind about something, nothing can change it."

"That's a comforting thought." Julia took a drink of the soda, then set the glass down on the table in front of her. "I don't know what to do, Amanda. What he's doing now goes beyond stubborn. He won't even discuss the possibility that the fertility tests he had done a few years ago were wrong."

Julia had come to Amanda the morning after Max's big announcement, so her friend had already been sworn to secrecy.

"I still don't know what to tell you about this." Amanda tucked her long legs up under her and shook her head. "You can't *make* him believe you."

"But he should. I mean, if I were lying," Julia said, jumping up out of her chair to pace, "wouldn't that have been the time for me to confess all? I mean, seriously, why would I keep insisting he's the father of the baby if he's not and I knew he wasn't? Does that make sense?" She stopped, shook her head, then rubbed at her temples. "I swear, sometimes I think I'm just going around and around in circles."

"Honey, you guys hardly know each other. It's no big surprise that he won't take your word for something as important as this."

"That's the point, though! I told him to go get retested, but he won't even discuss it. Says there's no reason for it."

"Stubborn, as already stated," Amanda said, giving her a supportive smile. "But I don't see what you can do about it."

"I can't, either." Julia huffed out a frustrated breath and shrugged. "I guess I just needed to rant."

"Nothing wrong with a good rant," Amanda told her. "And I'm always happy to listen. But—" she reached for a manila folder on the tabletop "—if you're finished for the moment, we could go over the last-minute details of the wedding."

The wedding. In a few days, she'd be marrying a man who was convinced she was a liar. How could that possibly be a good thing?

"Uh-oh," Amanda said softly. "I'm seeing hesitation in your eyes. Changing your mind about getting married? 'Cause if you are, tell me now so I can start the cancellations."

"No." Julia's head snapped up and her gaze fixed on her friend. "I'm not backing out." She laid one hand on her belly, as if she could comfort the child within. "No matter what he thinks, Max *is* the father of my baby. And my child deserves to have his father's name."

"True." Amanda tipped her head to one side and stared at her. "But what about *you?* Don't you deserve better than what Max is offering, Jules? Don't you deserve a man who trusts you? Loves you?"

Yes, she did. Julia's heart gave a little ping of pain. She wasn't foolish enough to think that Max loved her. But she knew he cared for her. He couldn't be as protective and supportive if he didn't feel *something* for her. And if he felt something, then he could eventually love her, right? After all, once the baby was born, she could insist on a paternity test. Then he'd know. Then he'd believe. But, God, she wished he could trust her without proof. Wished he could look into her eyes and see that she wouldn't lie to him about this.

Shaking her head, she walked back to her chair, dropped into it and said, "I deserve to marry the man *I* love. And I do love him—not that he'd believe me if I told him so," she added ruefully. Then her eyes narrowed, her chin lifted and her spine stiffened with determination. "But somehow, someday, I'm going to get through to the big jerk. And when that day comes, he's going to have to do some serious groveling to convince me to forgive him."

"Attagirl," Amanda said with a wide grin. "If anyone can do it, you can. Besides, there's nothing better than a good grovel."

"Any news on the blackmail front?"

Max lifted his head and shot a look at Alex. His friend had brought over some legal documents concerning the apartment building Max had just purchased. But now that their business was complete, Alex seemed in no hurry to leave.

"No, nothing. I spoke with Detective McGray yesterday and he says they have no leads. The blackmailer could have been anyone. But whoever it was is smart enough to leave no fingerprints on the notes left in Julia's mailbox."

Alex snorted a laugh. "That could be anyone who watches a crime show on television."

"True." Max leaned back in his leather chair and folded his hands across his middle. "According to the detective, they don't have anything new on that woman who died at 721, either."

Frowning, Alex said, "Seems unbelievable that a woman could die and leave no clues as to why."

"I know," Max said, glad that Julia had moved out of 721. He much preferred her living at his place, where he knew she was safe. There was definitely something not right going on at 721 and until the police discovered just what it was, Max thought no one would really be safe there.

"Poor woman," Alex said.

Max nodded. "McGray says that without more information, the police simply have nothing to go on."

"Must make you feel more relaxed having Julia out of there."

His words were so close to Max's thoughts it was a little disconcerting. His friend really knew him well.

"Got the invite to your wedding in the mail," Alex

said abruptly, as if deliberately steering them away from the troubling conversation.

"Yeah?"

"Still can't believe you're going to do this. I seem to remember that after Camille left, you vowed to never again step into the marriage 'bear trap,' I believe you called it."

"Things change."

"Uh-huh," Alex said wryly. "Though I've got to say I've seen happier bridegrooms. Hell, I've seen happier death-row inmates."

One of Max's eyebrows lifted and he sat forward, leaning his forearms on the pristine desktop. "What's to be happy about? This is a business deal, pure and simple."

"Sure it is."

"What's that supposed to mean?"

Alex laughed shortly. "You can try to fool yourself, man. But you're not fooling me."

"Is that right?"

"You forget, I've seen you two together."

"So?" Max shifted uncomfortably in his seat.

"So I've seen the way you look at her." Alex grinned and it was clearly the smile of an unattached man enjoying the sight of his friend being tied up in knots.

Irritated and just a little disgusted, Max stared at his friend. What the hell was going on lately? Was he losing his famous poker face? "I don't know what you're talking about."

"You don't want to know, you mean." Alex smiled and said, "You care about her."

"Don't be ridiculous." Despite the tension slowly coiling inside him, Max scoffed at his friend's statement. "You drew up the papers. You know damn well this is an arranged marriage. A convenience for both Julia and me."

"I know that's how it started."

Max stood up, turned his back on Alex and stared out the window at the sprawl of Manhattan beyond. Everything in him felt so tight it was a wonder he could breathe. Hearing Alex say he'd noticed Max's feelings only made this harder all the way around. He was a man who prided himself on keeping what he was thinking, feeling, to himself. The fact that his mask was slipping bothered him more than he could say.

"Hey, I don't blame you. Julia's great."

Yes, she was, Max thought, as unwillingly, his mind drew up an image of her, big blue eyes shining, delectable mouth curved in a smile, arms open to welcome him. Something inside him stirred and he had to fight for the control that had once been so easy to manage. But he'd noticed lately that control was a slippery thing for him. One thought of her and his body took over.

Julia had wormed herself into his life, his heart, and now he wasn't at all sure that he could manage to keep the careful distance between them he believed was so necessary.

He wouldn't allow himself to feel more for her than he already did. She was lying to him about something so elemental, it couldn't be overlooked. And despite being faced with facts, she refused to surrender the lie.

What did that say about her?

And what did it say about *him* that he was willing to put up with it?

"She's still lying to me," he muttered, more to himself than to Alex.

"Maybe she's not."

Max fixed him with a glare. His friend knew the truth. Knew why and how his marriage to Camille had ended. "We both know she is."

"We've talked about this before, Max."

"Yeah, we have, so let's skip it today, all right?"

"Fine." Alex held up both hands in mock surrender. "You've always been a stubborn son of a bitch."

Now Max laughed. "What's the old saying? Takes one to know one?"

Alex nodded. "Point taken," he said, then changed the subject. "Anyway, now that we've taken care of business and done the small-talk thing, how about we go get lunch?"

"Good idea." Pushing thoughts of Julia to the back of his mind where they'd simmer and burn, Max followed Alex out of the office.

Max found her in what would be the baby's room, painting the plain, beige walls a soft, restful green. She had earphones on and her hips were swaying to whatever music she was listening to. Her long, blond hair was tied back in a ponytail, her worn, faded jeans clung to her legs like a lover's hands and the hem of the T-shirt she wore stopped a couple of inches above the waistband of her jeans, displaying a ribbon of pale flesh.

He bit back a groan, leaned one shoulder against the doorjamb and folded his arms across his chest. With her back to him, she was completely unselfconscious. Her bare feet did intricate dance steps on the plastic covering the wood floor, and as she reached high to push the paint roller to the top of the wall, Max had to take a deep breath and hold it in an effort to steady himself.

He should go to her, he told himself. Take the roller out of her hands and tell her he'd hire someone to paint the damn room. She didn't have to do this herself. But as he listened to her soft voice singing, he realized she was enjoying herself and didn't want to take that from her.

When she turned to dip the roller into the paint tray behind her, she saw him, pulled off her earphones and shrieked. "Max! Why didn't you say something? Let me know you were there?"

"I was enjoying the show."

Her face flushed and she dipped her head before saying, "I, um…"

"You're a good dancer." He was enjoying her embarrassment. Hell, usually, she was so put together, so in control, it was a nice change to catch her unawares.

She smiled at him and said, "Yeah, I'm going to try out for the Rockettes next year."

"You've got my vote." She had paint drops speckling her cheeks and a streak of green across her forehead. Max reached out and rubbed at that streak with his thumb. "You've also got paint on your face."

"Great." She laughed, rolled her eyes and said, "But the room looks good, doesn't it?"

"Yeah," he said, his gaze locked with hers. "It does. But you should have told me you wanted to do this, Julia. I could have gotten a team of painters in here to—"

"I wanted to do it myself," she said quickly. "It's important to me, Max. I want our baby to feel welcome from the very beginning."

Our baby, he thought, as something twisted around his heart. He'd give a lot for that to be reality. To actually *be* this baby's father in more than name. Startling himself with the force of that wayward thought, Max put it aside. "He can be welcome without you wielding a paint roller yourself."

She set the roller down on the tray and peeled off the plastic gloves she'd been wearing to protect her hands. Smoothing her hair at the sides of her head, she said only, "I wanted to do it."

"Okay," he said, then asked, "you planning on painting the connecting room for a nanny?"

She shot him a quick look. "No nannies. No helpers. I don't want strangers raising my child."

"Good," he said, nodding as he pulled her up close. "I don't want that, either."

"Max." She tried to pull back. "I'll get paint on your suit."

"Doesn't matter," he said, his gaze moving over her,

his hands lifting to cup her face. Heat rushed through him with an intensity he was becoming all too used to. "I've got lots of suits." His fingers moved over the frecklelike specks of paint on her cheeks. "Green looks good on you."

"I bet you say that to all your fiancées."

"Only the pregnant ones."

And then he kissed her, pushing his doubts and worries out of his mind to be drowned in the rising tide of passion.

Eleven

A week later the wedding went off without a hitch.

Julia wore a floor-length, strapless ivory gown, and felt like a princess standing beside her very handsome groom in a three-piece black suit. The dozen or so guests were all close friends and thankfully, there'd been no last-minute crises.

Her parents didn't attend the wedding, for which Julia was extremely grateful. She didn't want or need anything to distract her from the jumble of feelings already charging through her system.

The judge, a friend of Max's, conducted the brief civil ceremony in Max's penthouse with an easy friendliness that should have eased Julia's nerves. But standing there beside Max as the judge talked about cherishing and loving and till death did them part, all Julia could think was, *What if I'm making the biggest mistake of my life?*

Stupid, no doubt, to be thinking about that now. But she couldn't help herself. She loved Max, but she was beginning to doubt that he would ever allow himself to love her in return. Even now, as they stood together thanking their guests for coming, she felt a distance between them. Felt him holding himself apart.

She'd hoped somehow that actually getting married would dissolve some of Max's detachment. That once they'd made the legal commitment to each other he would permit himself to form at least a tenuous connection with her. But so far, anyway, she'd seen no sign of that and her heart ached a little—for herself and her child.

She wanted a family. She'd always wanted to build the kind of family she'd dreamed of as a child. And she knew that if Max would just let her in, they could have everything she'd ever dreamed of and more.

"Where are you?"

Max's whisper came against her ear, startling her out of her thoughts. Julia turned her face up to his and gave him a smile. "Just thinking."

"From your expression, not very happy thoughts," he said, keeping his voice low enough that only she could hear him.

"Sorry," she said, and meant it. She didn't want Max or anyone else thinking that she was having second thoughts. "I guess it's all just a little overwhelming."

He nodded and stepped in front of her, turning his back to the crowd, cutting her off from anyone who might be interested enough to watch them. "I know this was fast, but we're both getting what we want, right?"

Some of what we want, anyway, she told herself as she looked up into his green eyes.

"So let's just get through the reception and then we can relax."

"You're right," she said, and smiled more brightly, forcing a cheerfulness she didn't feel.

"Hey," Alex said as he came up behind Max and tapped him on the shoulder, "no hogging the bride. According to tradition, I get to claim a kiss."

Max swiveled his head to give his friend a dirty look. "Since when are you traditional?"

"Since I want to kiss a beautiful woman without her new husband decking me for it."

Julia laughed at the look of consternation on Max's face and took some heart in the fact that he clearly didn't want to share her. That was something, right? Stepping around her new husband, she smiled at Alex. "Far be it from us to defy tradition."

Almost as handsome as Max, Alex gave her a smile that let her know he understood that she must be having mixed feelings about the ceremony. Then he stepped in close, leaned down and kissed her hard and fast.

There was no *zip* in the contact, just a feeling of warmth and support. Especially when Alex paused long enough to whisper, "Be patient. He'll come around."

Before she could say anything to that, though, Max was tugging his friend away and saying, "One kiss per customer. Move it."

Alex only laughed and tucked his hands into the pockets of his slacks. "Fine, fine. Be greedy. Guess I'll just have to go and find a different girl." He swept the small crowd with a keen eye, then suddenly narrowed his gaze. "Like that one, for instance," he said softly.

He was gone before Julia could see who he was talking about, and then Max was turning her into his arms and she forgot all about their guests. "I didn't get a kiss from the bride yet."

"Yes, you did," she said, smiling up at him. "At the end of the ceremony."

"That one was for everyone else," he told her, already dipping his head down to hers. "This one's for me."

His mouth took hers and the world fell away. Julia's heartbeat quickened and every cell in her body lit up in celebration. Would it always be like this? she wondered.

She leaned into him, giving him everything she had, willing him to read the truth in her kiss. Willing him to sense that she was offering him her love. Willing him to *want* it.

When he lifted his head finally and she saw the dark gleam in his eyes, she knew desire was thrumming through him.

He lifted one hand, touched her cheek, then smoothed his thumb across her bottom lip. "Did I tell you today that you make a beautiful bride?"

"No, but thank you."

"I want you to know…" Max stopped, caught in the onslaught of feelings that were crashing together inside him. From the moment she'd stepped out of the master bedroom to walk to him down a short, makeshift aisle, he hadn't been able to see anything but her. It was as if no one else in the room existed. She was everything.

Her eyes were the color of a summer sky. Her mouth was curved in a soft smile. Her hands were cupped around a bouquet of pale pink peonies, and fragile sandals were strapped to her small, delicate feet. She was the picture of what every bride should look like and all Max could think was *She's mine*.

He knew the taste of her, the feel of her beneath him, the satin of her skin under his palms. He knew how she danced when she thought no one was looking, and he'd seen the hurt in her eyes when her own mother had turned on her. Her laughter warmed him and her tears cut him off at the knees.

She'd become…important to him. She'd become a part of his days, his nights, his life. And that realization staggered him. He hadn't planned for this. Hadn't expected to care. Hadn't *wanted* to care.

He had to find a way to stop.

"What, Max?" Julia reached for him, the sapphire-and-diamond ring he'd just given her flashing on her left hand. "What did you want me to know?"

He shook himself, as if he'd just stumbled in out of a summer storm. Deliberately, he sent those tender feelings he was experiencing flying from him like unwanted raindrops. His brain struggled to keep up and he tried to remember what he'd been about to say to her. Damned if he could. Which was probably just as well, since a moment or two ago, he'd been in the grips of an emotional whirlwind he wanted no part of.

"Nothing," he said, retreating into the cool, dispassionate world he felt so much more comfortable in. He gave her a smile that never reached his eyes and said, "It was nothing at all."

Julia didn't spend another moment alone with Max for the rest of the afternoon. It seemed that every time she came near him, he found someone else to speak to—usually on the other side of the room.

Several of their guests had already left and as the reception wound down, Julia noticed Amanda and Alex standing in a corner. They looked striking together, and judging by the animated way Amanda's hands moved as she spoke, they were finding plenty to talk about. Was Amanda the woman Alex had seemed so interested in before? Julia hoped so. Her best friend was due some good luck with men after having had such a worm for her ex-boyfriend.

"It was a great party," someone said from close by, and Julia turned to smile at Carrie Gray. "And you make a gorgeous bride, which I'm trying not to hold against you."

Julia laughed, hugged her friend and said, "Thanks for coming, Carrie. I really appreciate it."

"Are you kidding? Wouldn't have missed it." Carrie

stepped back, slung her purse strap over her shoulder and asked, "So where are you going on your honeymoon, or is that a state secret?"

"No honeymoon," Julia said. "We're both so busy right now…" She let her voice trail off, hoping Carrie wouldn't hear the disappointment.

"Well, that's a shame," Carrie said, pouting. "Doesn't seem fair, does it? Well, maybe you two can sneak off in a month or so."

"Maybe," Julia said, and waved as Carrie left. Max hadn't wanted a honeymoon. He said that there would be no point since this wasn't exactly a conventional marriage.

One by one, the other guests trickled from the penthouse, until only she, Max, Amanda and Alex were left.

"It was a great wedding if I do say so myself," Amanda said, smiling as she gave Julia a big hug.

"You outdid yourself and on really short notice, too," Julia told her. "I don't know what I would have done if you hadn't planned all of this with me."

Amanda looked great in a dark red sundress with short sleeves and a full skirt. Her short blond hair was ruffled, as always, since Amanda tended to run her hands through it a lot. But her big gray eyes were shining as she said, "What do you think of Max's friend Alex?"

"I like him. He's nice. Ambitious. Funny."

"Hmm." Amanda sent a quick look to where Max and Alex were talking together.

"You interested?" Julia asked.

"I'm not *not* interested," Amanda said. Then she shrugged and grinned. "Anyway, I'm heading out. I just wanted to say be happy, honey. And if you ever need anything, you know where to find me."

"I do."

"Hey, you're getting really good at that phrase."

Julia laughed, hugged her best friend again, then wistfully watched her stride across the room with a wave for Max before heading out to the elevator. Alex left right on her heels and Julia silently wished Amanda luck.

"So," Max said as he walked toward her, "the deed is done."

"It certainly is." She rubbed her thumb across her shiny new wedding ring.

The sunlight coming through the bank of windows was diffused slightly by the tinted glass, but still the light hit Max like gold, making his green eyes shine as if lit from within. When he came closer and reached for her, Julia went willingly. He was her husband. She loved him. And for just today, anyway, she was going to let go of the niggling doubts and worries gnawing at her mind and do what every other bride was entitled to do.

Make love with her groom.

A few days later Max sat in on a meeting with investors and found his mind wandering. Until Julia, that had never happened to him. Now, though, instead of concentrating on spreadsheets and financial predictions, his mind insisted on turning to images of his wife.

His *wife*.

While one of his employees ran through a presentation, Max's gaze dropped to the plain gold band on his left hand. He'd never thought to wear one of those again. Had never wanted to.

Now, like it or not, he was a husband.

The past few days hadn't been easy. Julia was already so firmly entrenched in his life, Max had to wonder how he would let her go at the end of the year. That worried him. He couldn't trust her, damn it, and how the hell could he stay married to a woman he didn't trust?

But could he stand watching her walk away? His thoughts idly drifted to that morning, gathering Julia's warm, naked, pliant body against his, filling his hands with her breasts, burying himself deep inside her. And as he remembered, so did his body, until he was uncomfortably hard in the middle of a damned meeting.

Scowling, he tapped a pencil atop the long, walnut table and only stopped when he saw a flicker of unease in one of his vice president's eyes. Tossing the pencil down, he forced himself to pay attention and couldn't figure out how it had come to this. He'd *always* been on top of his business. Always had his fingertips on the pulse of Wall Street. Always ran the meetings at his company with an iron fist and a steely eye. He'd never zoned out, even when he was married before.

But then, Camille hadn't haunted him morning and night as Julia did. Julia and her lies. His back teeth ground together and when the lights in the conference room clicked off for a slide show, he was grateful for the darkness.

In the shadows, Max could silently admit that he actually wanted to believe in Julia. Wanted to trust her. But how the hell could he? He'd seen the results of the fertility tests his ex-wife had insisted on.

As his employees' voices droned around him, Max frowned again, thinking of his ex. Camille had made him pay through the nose in their divorce settlement *because* he was infertile and she couldn't have the child she'd wanted.

That old sense of failure settled in his chest like an cold rock and he rubbed at the spot as if he could make it disappear. But the icy sensation remained. There was only one thing he could do. He had to pull back from Julia, from what he was feeling. It was better that way.

For both of them.

Several hours later Julia was still waiting dinner for Max. He was supposed to have been home two hours ago, but hadn't shown up. Or called. She walked to the bank of windows overlooking the city and stared down at the tiny cars and the sea of tiny people hurtling along the crowded streets. *Where is he?*

A glance at the table behind her sent pain jolting through her. The white tapers were burned halfway down and the breathing red wine had inhaled so much air it probably wasn't any good anymore. She blew out a sigh and decided to be annoyed rather than sad.

"Why didn't he at least call?" she muttered aloud, then another thought hit. "What if he *can't* call? What if he was in an accident? What if he was run down in the street by a careening cab? What if…" She stopped talking and moved to the phone in the living room.

Dropping onto the nearby couch, she lifted the wireless receiver, punched in Max's work number and waited. Three rings later, his familiar, deep voice said, "Rolland."

"Max?" Relief swept her first. He wasn't dead in the street. But he could be dead, anyway, in a minute or two! "You're still at work?"

"Obviously."

That single word was clipped and cool and about as friendly as a kiss from a polar bear. She curled her legs under her and wrapped one arm around her middle. "Is there something wrong?"

"No," he said. "What're you calling for? Did you need something?"

Julia sucked in air and held it for a second. Over the past few days, she'd almost convinced herself that she and Max were going to be able to make something of this marriage. She'd pretended that he was warming to her. That he eagerly reached for her every night because he was coming to care for her.

Clearly, she'd been fooling herself.

"I was worried," she admitted a moment later, her voice soft. "Dinner was ready a couple of hours ago and when I didn't hear from you I—"

His impatient huff came through the phone loud and clear and hit her like a slap.

"Julia, don't do this."

"Do what?"

"Act the part of the aggrieved wife," he said, voice clipped and dispassionate. "We're married, yes, and we have to keep up a good front for our friends. But you and I know the truth."

"Which is?" Her hand on the receiver tightened as her gaze fixed on a tall porcelain vase across the room that only that morning she'd filled with summer flowers.

"That all we've got between us is a carefully worded business deal and some great sex."

"Max—"

"You needed help," he said. "I needed an heir, so I'm accepting another man's child as my own. Period."

Pain lanced her, but as quickly as it appeared, it tangled with a quiet fury.

"You'll never believe me, will you," she said, speaking more to herself than to him.

"No."

"Not even when the baby is born and I can provide you with a paternity test, you still won't believe. You'll still doubt me. You'll probably accuse me of falsifying the test."

"Don't do this, Julia."

"I'm not the one doing this, Max." She unfolded her legs, stood up and scooped one hand through her oh-so-carefully arranged hair. She glanced down at the slinky, dark green dress she'd worn just for him and told herself she was all kinds of fool.

"Julia…"

She desperately pulled in air because she felt as though she'd never be able to breathe easily again. Her lungs were tight, her heart was aching and her hands were shaking with repressed anger.

"I'm leaving, Max."

"What?"

How strange, she thought, to be doing this over the phone. But even as she thought it, she realized that it was a very appropriate goodbye to a marriage that had never promised more than distance between the very people it should have joined.

"I'm leaving. I can't do this," she said, already walking toward their bedroom, the phone clutched tightly in one hand. She paused at the dining-room table long enough to blow out the candles, then idly watched as spirals of gray smoke rose and twisted in the chill of the air-conditioned room.

She thought about breaking the wine bottle, pulling the Irish-linen tablecloth off the table and scattering the Limoges china across the wood floor, but didn't. And points for her. Continuing on to the bedroom, she listened to Max, still speaking calmly.

"We have a signed agreement between us," he said.

"Sue me."

"Damn it, Julia…"

"I thought I could do it," she said, assuring herself that she was making the right decision. "I really thought

I could. I thought *we* could make this marriage work. But as long as you continue to believe the worst of me, we don't stand a chance."

"You can't leave."

"Oh, yes I can." She should hang up. Hang up, pack and get out. But for some damn reason, she couldn't bring herself to hit the end button on the phone. She didn't want to shut his voice off. "I'm sorry, Max," she said softly. "For both of us. But I can't remain married to a man who thinks so little of me, and I will not allow my child to grow up feeling his father's innate rejection every day. I was forced to do that myself and the pain is something that's still with me."

Max had eased it a little, she remembered, but now that was done, too, and she wouldn't have him in her corner when dealing with her parents anymore.

"I told you I would love your child."

"He's *ours,* Max." Julia yanked at her hair in frustration, then muttered, "I should have known this was a bad idea. My fault. Entirely my fault."

"And the blackmailer?"

"I'll be a divorced woman. Nothing to blackmail me with."

"Damn it, Julia. I can be home in twenty minutes. We can talk about this in person."

"No," she said, gathering up handfuls of underwear, bras and whatever else she could grab quickly. Not caring about neatness, she tossed it all into the suitcase, she wasn't worried about neatness, she headed for the closet again. Yanking down a few shirts and pairs of slacks, she carried them one-handed to the suitcase and tossed them in, too. She could come back for the rest. Or not. Maybe she'd just buy all new stuff.

As she zipped the case closed, she dropped onto the edge of the bed and said, "You know what the saddest part of this is, Max? I actually love you."

"What?"

A short, sharp laugh shot from her throat. Julia turned her head to the view outside the bedroom window and concentrated on the sea of city lights spreading out into the distance. "Yeah, it surprised me, too. After all, how could any rational, logical woman love a man who's too stubborn to change? Too filled with anger to see that sometimes things aren't what they seem?" She stood up, grabbed the suitcase and pulled it off the bed. "How can I possibly love a man who's too arrogant to acknowledge that maybe, just maybe, he isn't right about everything?"

"Julia—"

"Goodbye, Max." She punched end, tossed the phone onto the bed and walked out of the apartment, out of Max's life, forever.

Twelve

The next few days crawled past.

Max didn't race home after Julia's phone call. Mainly because he'd assured himself she was bluffing. When he finally strolled in hours later, he was alone in the suddenly too-big loft penthouse. Even then, though, he had told himself that it was for the best. He'd begun to care too much for her. Having her leave was the best thing that could have happened.

Besides, because of the legal papers she'd signed, he still had a claim on her and her child, which meant she wouldn't be getting rid of him as easily as she'd supposed.

He left the apartment at dawn every day and stayed late at the office every night. He told himself it was because he was free to devote as much of his time to his work as he wanted. But the truth was, he hated the silence in his apartment. He hated that he could still hear the echoes of her laughter, her sighs, her soft whispers in the night. He hated that her clothes were still in the closet and just the act of his choosing a suit every morning meant he was assailed by her scent. He hated that he'd left the high heels she'd kicked off on her last day in the apartment right where they'd landed on the floor at her side of the bed.

And he really hated that he hated all of that.

He shouldn't care.

Should be glad to have his own life back the way he wanted it.

He wasn't, though, but he'd be damned if he'd go racing after her. He'd done the right thing by her. He'd married her, offered to take her child as his own. He'd protected her from a blackmailer, gotten her out of an apartment building that might not be safe, and all he'd asked in return was the truth.

She'd refused to give it to him, instead, clinging to her lie. It was a *lie*, wasn't it?

"You're thinking about her again."

Max jolted out of his thoughts and shifted a hard look to Alex, sitting across the linen-draped table from him. Their weekly lunch was over, the servers had cleared the dishes, leaving only two steaming cups of black coffee behind. Max didn't answer, just picked up his coffee and took a swallow, the hot liquid searing his esophagus.

"I did some checking," Alex was saying, idly turning his coffee cup in its saucer, the china making a low singing scrape as it moved on itself.

"Into what?" Max set his cup down with a click of sound.

"Into Julia's ex-boyfriend. You know he's an attorney at my firm."

Max scowled at him.

Alex ignored it. "Turns out, Julia and he were nothing more than good friends the last few months they were together. No sex. No chance that he's the father of her baby." Alex lifted his coffee cup to take a sip, but paused long enough to say, "Seems the only man she slept with was you."

The tension in Max's body tightened perceptibly, but he shrugged off Alex's words. "Doesn't matter what that guy says. Camille showed me the fertility reports."

"Right." Alex set his cup down, braced his forearms on the table and glared at Max. "In case you've forgotten, let me be the first to remind you that Camille was a bitch."

Max sighed. "Agreed."

"So why is it you're willing to take Camille's word over Julia's for anything?"

"Good point." Max took a breath, gritted his teeth and asked himself if he'd been a complete ass. He'd turned away from Julia, refusing to listen to her, believe her, because Camille had turned him inside out. What if his ex was the one lying to him? What if Julia was right and Camille had somehow forged the results of that test? What if he'd had everything he'd ever really wanted and let it slip through his fingers because he'd been too arrogant to admit he might have been wrong?

"Judging by the look in your eyes," Alex mused, "I think you've just had an epiphany."

"Maybe I have," Max admitted, lifting one hand to signal the waiter.

"Never mind," Alex told him. "I'll get lunch."

"Thanks." He slid out of the leather booth. "I've got to check something out."

"'Bout time."

"Yeah, yeah." Max shot his friend a tight smile as he felt the first stirrings of hope.

"Hey, before you go…"

Max looked at him.

"How about giving me Julia's friend Amanda's phone number?"

Max grinned. "Get your own girl. I've got problems of my own to worry about."

"You've got to get out of the apartment," Amanda said.

"I know, don't worry." Julia snuggled deeper into the armchair in Amanda's living room. She hadn't wanted to crash back at her old apartment with her best friend, but she'd had nowhere else to go when she left Max's place. She certainly couldn't go to her parents'. And she hadn't wanted to be alone in an impersonal hotel room.

Amanda had been great, welcoming her back, staying up late every night to listen to Julia, torn between misery and fury, ramble on about Max. But she was right. Julia had to move out. She couldn't stay here. She'd have to find her own place.

"I'll see a Realtor tomorrow," she said. "Promise. I'll move out as soon as I can."

"You dope," Amanda said, dropping down onto the arm of the chair. "I didn't mean you had to *move* out. I meant you had to *get* out. Walk outside. Get some air."

"Oh." Feeling like an idiot, Julia smiled up at her friend. "You've been so nice, Amanda. Letting me stay. Letting me rant."

"What's a best friend for?" The tall, pretty blonde smiled. "But, Jules, honey, you've been locked away inside the apartment for four days. That's not healthy. Your skin's already pale. Much more sunlight deprivation, you're going to fade away completely."

"I just don't feel like seeing anybody," Julia said quietly, looking around the familiar and yet different apartment. Amanda had put her own stamp on the place in just a week or so. There were feminine touches everywhere. "I feel like I want to crawl into a hole and pull the hole in after me."

"Shame on you."

"What?" She looked up into Amanda's steady gray eyes.

"You're hiding, honey. And you didn't do anything wrong." She paused to scowl a little. "Well, except for falling in love with a man who clearly doesn't deserve you."

"I'm not hiding, I'm…regrouping." Just until she

got over Max. Shouldn't take her more than ten or twenty years.

Reaching out, Amanda patted her hand. "You know you're welcome to stay here however long you want."

"Thanks."

"But…"

"What?"

Amanda gave her a sad smile. "The truth is, you'll never be happy without Max. You're a one-man woman, sweetie, and he's yours."

When Amanda got up and walked to the kitchen, Julia sighed and fought the sting of tears in her eyes. Amanda was wrong. She had to be. Because Max didn't want her and Julia really didn't want to spend the rest of her life miserable.

"I need to see my test results," Max demanded, leaning against the edge of the doctor's desk. The office was cluttered, the air was cool and the older man smiling up at him seemed completely unperturbed by Max's presence.

"Of course, Mr. Rolland. There was really no need to bully my secretary."

"I'm in a hurry." God, was he in a hurry. If he was right and Camille had lied to him, he had a hell of a lot to make up for.

The doctor walked to a bank of file cabinets, opened one and flipped through the files until he found the one he wanted. Pulling it free, he handed it over. "As you'll see, the results are just as I told you two years ago."

Max stopped listening. There was a roaring in his ears as his blood rushed and pumped in a fury. He stared down at the test results and felt rage and relief tangle so tightly in his chest he could hardly draw a breath.

He wasn't infertile.

Camille had lied.

Julia was telling the truth.

And he was the biggest damn fool in the city.

Lifting his gaze to the doctor, he handed the file back, muttered, "Thank you," and left.

He hit the crowded Manhattan street and came to a dead stop as his brain raced. The summer sun beat down on the city and the humidity was so high a man could sweat to death standing still. But Max felt cold to the bone.

He'd had a chance at something real. Something lasting, with Julia and his child.

His child.

He closed his eyes, shook his head and cursed himself for being so stubborn, so arrogant. As pedestrians bumped into him as they passed, he remembered every moment he'd had with Julia. The ups, the downs, the lovemaking, the laughter and arguments, and he knew, with a certainty that reverberated in his soul, that she was the only woman in the world for him.

Now he had to find a way to convince her that he was a changed man. That he loved her. Opening his eyes, he stalked down the sidewalk like a man possessed and people scrambled to get out of his way.

* * *

When the doorbell rang, Amanda went to answer it. Max wasn't sure what her response to him would be, but it only took a second for her to grin at him. Well, why wouldn't she? He was standing in the hallway, holding a bouquet of flowers as big as a small child and no doubt had a haunted expression on his face.

"Who is it?" Julia shouted in the distance and Max's gaze shot in that direction.

"It's for you," Amanda called back, reaching out to grab her purse and sling it over her shoulder. "I'm running out for a latte. Be back in a bit." When she stepped past Max, she paused long enough to whisper, "Good luck."

He'd need it. Max closed the door after her and stood where he was until Julia walked into the room. One look at her and everything in him shifted, eased, as if an unseen chain around his heart and lungs had been released. She was more beautiful than ever, though her eyes looked wounded and wary. If he could have, he would have kicked his own ass for putting those emotions in her beautiful eyes, and he wondered if it was too late for him to fix this. But she hadn't turned away from him. Hadn't left the room. Surely that meant something.

"Julia…" He took a step and she moved backward.

"What do you want, Max?" She twisted her hands in front of her waist.

"You," he said simply. "I want you. Tell me I'm not too late. Tell me you still love me."

Her blue eyes widened and surprise flickered in their

depths, overshadowing the pain. When she didn't speak, didn't back farther away, Max walked closer, moving slowly, cautiously. He'd made his fortune by knowing which move to make when. What to say and who to say it to. Now, though, when he needed that instinctive sense of rightness, it had deserted him.

This was too important to screw up.

This conversation would set the course of his life. So he started at the top.

"I was wrong, Julia. So wrong about so many things. I should have believed you. Believed *in* you." In the reflected sunlight, he saw a sheen of tears on her eyes and it nearly killed him. "I'm so sorry, Julia. For everything."

Still she didn't speak and a panic like he'd never known before jolted him so hard he almost hit his knees. God, what he'd come to! He laughed shortly and the sound was a raw scrape of pain. "I never apologize. Ask anyone. So I'm not very good at it, but I'm trying, because you're too important to me."

"Since when?" she asked, her voice a hush of sound almost lost in the silent room. "Since when am I important to you, Max?"

"You always have been," he said, glancing at the flowers in his hands and wondering why he'd been stupid enough to think they would sway her. Tossing them onto the closest chair, he took another step toward her. Toward salvation. "From that first night. The first time I saw you. Touched you. I knew it. On a bone-deep level, I knew that you were the one for me. I just couldn't bring myself to admit it, I guess."

"Until now?" She shook her head and her soft blond hair moved over her shoulders like a caress. "Why now, Max?"

He told her everything. About Camille's lies. About the truth in the fertility reports. "You're carrying my baby, Julia, and I should have believed you. I'll never be able to make that up to you, I know. But I want to be with you. Want to love you. *And* our baby."

She moved to the side, inching a bit farther out of his reach and shook her head again. Her eyes gleamed at him like shards of broken turquoise. "I'd like to believe you, Max, you don't know how much. But I know now I'll never be satisfied being with you just because of our baby. I want your heart, Max. I want it all. Or I want nothing."

"You have it," he said, moving so fast, it surprised even him. He took hold of her shoulders, pulled her close to him and looked down into the blue eyes that had haunted him from the moment he'd first seen them. "You have my love. You have *me*. I'm no damn prize, Julia. I know that. But I guarantee you no man will ever love you as much as I do."

A single tear escaped her right eye and disappeared into the soft blond hair at her temple. "Max…"

"Julia," he said softly, stroking her face, her hair, "there's only one person in the world who could bring Max Rolland to his knees. The woman I love."

"What?"

Keeping his gaze locked with hers, Max dropped to

one knee in front of her. Picking up her left hand, he kissed the wedding ring he'd placed on her finger only days before, then looked up into her shining eyes.

"Give me another chance, Julia. Let me love you as you should be loved. Let me be a part of your life. Let me help you raise our children." His thumb smoothed over her knuckles. "Let me inside you, Julia. And never let me go."

She bit her bottom lip as tears began to rain down her face. Then she laughed a little and Max took his first easy breath in days. She hadn't turned her back on him. She was smiling at him.

"Get up, Max."

He did, and taking those tears and her smile to heart, he pulled her against him again, relishing the warm softness of her. The strength in her. She was everything he'd always wanted and so much more.

She was, quite simply, everything.

"Will you come home with me?" he asked, kissing her forehead, her cheeks. "Now?"

"Answer one question first," she said, pulling back to look up at him.

Uneasiness whipped through him, then dissolved as he saw the gleam of happiness in her eyes. "Anything."

Her hand cupped his cheek. "You said you wanted me to let you help raise our *children*. How many did you have in mind?"

He laughed for the first time in what felt like forever and peace showered down on him like a warm summer rain. Holding on to her as if it meant his life, he whispered, "As many as we want, my love. As many as we want."

Then he kissed her and felt his life, his world, come right again.

* * * * *

LAURA WRIGHT

FRONT PAGE ENGAGEMENT

Media mogul and playboy Trent Tanford is being blackmailed *and* he's involved in a scandal. Needing to shed his image, Trent marries his girl-next-door neighbor, Carrie Gray, with some major cash tossed her way. Carrie accepts for her own reasons, but falls in love with Trent and wonders if he could feel the same way about her— even though their mock marriage was, after all, just a business deal.

**Available August
wherever books are sold.**

Always Powerful, Passionate and Provocative.

Harlequin® Historical
Historical Romantic Adventure!

From *USA TODAY*
bestselling author
Margaret Moore

A LOVER'S KISS

A Frenchwoman in London,
Juliette Bergerine is unexpectedly
thrown together in hiding with
Sir Douglas Drury. As lust and
desire give way to deeper emotions,
how will Juliette react on discovering
that her brother was murdered—
by Drury!

*Available September
wherever you buy books.*

HH29508

KATHERINE GARBERA
BABY BUSINESS

Cassidy Franzone wants Donovan Tolley,
one of South Carolina's most prestigious
and eligible bachelors. But when she
becomes pregnant with his heir, she is
furious that Donovan uses her and their
child to take over the family business.
Convincing his pregnant ex-fiancée to marry
him now will take all his negotiating
skills, but the greatest risk he faces is
falling for her for real.

**Available August
wherever books are sold.**

Always Powerful, Passionate and Provocative.

COMING NEXT MONTH

#1885 FRONT PAGE ENGAGEMENT—Laura Wright
Park Avenue Scandals
This media mogul needs to shed his playboy image, and who better to tame his wild ways than his sexy girl-next-door neighbor?

#1886 BILLIONAIRE'S MARRIAGE BARGAIN—
Leanne Banks
The Billionaires Club
Marry his investor's daughter and he'd have unlimited business backing. Then he discovered that his convenient fiancée was passion personified...and all bets were off.

#1887 WED TO THE TEXAN—Sara Orwig
Platinum Grooms
They were only to be married for one year, but this Texas billionaire wasn't through with his pretend wife just yet.

#1888 BABY BUSINESS—Katherine Garbera
Billionaires and Babies
Convincing his pregnant ex-fiancée to marry him will take all his negotiating skills. Falling for her for real...that will be his greatest risk.

#1889 FIVE-STAR COWBOY—Charlene Sands
Suite Secrets
He wants her in his boardroom and his bedroom, and when this millionaire cowboy realizes she's the answer to his business needs...seduction unfolds.

#1890 CLAIMING HIS RUNAWAY BRIDE—
Yvonne Lindsay
An accident leaves her without any memories of the past. Then a handsome man appears at her door claiming she's his wife....